PUFFIN BO

Little Mother Meg

Life ripples on at Misrule, as the children grow older and a grandchild is born.

But not everything is straightforward. While Bunty and Poppet journey to Meg's house on their prized bicycles, little Peter and Essie find adventure and mystery much closer to home . . .

The children may be older but the world of Misrule, the rambling home of the Woolcot family, is still as welcoming as ever. Loved by readers everywhere in *Seven Little Australians*, this famous Australian family comes to us in another classic story.

Little Mother Meg is one of four books in Ethel Turner's timeless series, which includes *Seven Little Australians*, *The Family at Misrule* and *Judy and Punch*.

Ethel Turner and her daughter, Jean, aged 13 months.

Little Mother Meg

Ethel Turner

PUFFIN BOOKS

Puffin Books
Penguin Books Australia Ltd
487 Maroondah Highway, PO Box 257
Ringwood, Victoria 3134, Australia
Penguin Books Ltd
Harmondsworth, Middlesex, England
Viking Penguin, A Division of Penguin Books USA Inc.
375 Hudson Street, New York, New York 10014, USA
Penguin Books Canada Limited
10 Alcorn Avenue, Toronto, Ontario, Canada M4V 3B2
Penguin Books (N.Z.) Ltd
Cnr Rosedale and Airborne Roads, Albany, Auckland

First published by Ward Lock, 1902
This paperback edition published by Penguin Books Australia, 1997
1 3 5 7 9 10 8 6 4 2
Copyright © Philippa Poole, 1997

Typeset in 12/14 pt Berkeley Old Style by Midland Typesetters, Maryborough, Victoria
Made and printed in Australia by Australian Print Group, Maryborough, Victoria

National Library of Australia
Cataloguing-in-Publication data:

Turner, Ethel, 1870–1958.
Little mother Meg.

ISBN 0 14 034727 5.

I. Title.

A823.2

Contents

To
ROSIE

CHAPTER ONE

'Going to Meg's'

There was the freshness of early winter in the air. The river leaped and laughed in its old brown rocky bed, the autumn rains had washed the summer brown from the grassed banks and coloured them so sweetly green you would have thought that Spring herself had passed over them with twinkling feet.

Even the gum-trees could not quite make up their minds as to the season. There stood a group with trunks so richly red and brown, that to a boat shooting round the river bend all the landscape directly in front seemed suffused with the royal autumn tints.

But here a tongue of land that ran out into the water was thick with young wattle bursting into leaves of spring-like greenness.

And if the eye looked ahead, far, far up the river where Misrule's paddocks ran down wild-haired to the waters, the tree-trunks there, as if to accentuate the irresolute note of nature, gleamed white as silver.

Down in the tumble-down boat shed at the edge of the poppy paddock Bunty was drying out the boat, and putting in the gay red cushions. He was working not cheerfully but of necessity.

It was Saturday afternoon, and after the early dinner customary to that day of the week, he had said he was going down to Meg's, and went off whistling across the grass. Peter came bursting down after him. 'Wait for me, wait for me – I'm coming too,' he shouted. Bunty was standing up in the boat and pushing off, but at the shout he steadied the little craft a second.

'Jump, then,' he called out, and Peter leaped wildly after him, and landed in a pool in the bottom of the boat.

'Why didn't you bale her out?' the small youth said, his spirits a trifle saddened at the sight of his wet boots and the splashes on the clean cuffs of his sailor blouse. 'Aren't you going to? There's a bucket of water there at least.'

'You let it alone and it'll let you alone,' quoth Bunty laconically. 'Stick your feet on the seat or sit on them or something, if they get in your road.'

Over the grass came yet another flying figure – eager little Essie, five now, with browny-gold curls streaming out behind her, and scarlet on her cheeks and sparkles in her round brown eyes.

'Stop, stop,' she shouted, 'you're to stop – do you hear! Stop at once – Nellie says.'

'Oh, hang,' said Bunty, 'now what's to pay?'

'We can't come back,' shouted Peter; 'go away – go home at once, Essie, we can't take you, the boat's as wet as sop.'

But Essie continued to shout and gesticulate so energetically that Bunty took an unwilling back-stroke or two.

Nellie wanted to come – that was the substance of the message – Nellie herself intended to go down to Meg's this afternoon, and Bunty would please to see the boat was dry and fit to go in.

So Bunty came back and tied the boat up again, not over cheerfully, and baled out the water with an ox-tongue tin, and mopped the seats dry.

'Cut up to the house and get a rug, Jumbo,' he said, 'and the cushions are in the coach house; I put them there because the shed leaks.'

Peter went off to obey the mandate, and Essie insisted upon helping to bale out. She got a rusty pannikin from the picnic hamper and baled vigorously, spilling the water naturally down the front of her muslin pinafore.

Then Poppet appeared – Poppet at twelve grown strangely, almost painfully, like Judy, bright little eager-eyed Judy on whose far-off, quiet grave the suns had shone and the grey rains fallen for more than eight long years.

And last of all came Nell – Nell just nineteen, Nell in a dress of deep heliotrope shade, with a black velvet picture-hat setting off her fresh young beauty.

But now what was to be done? The big boat was up, high and dry, waiting for repairs. This little dinghy Bunty had prepared was meant for two, but would hold three at a pinch. And five of them were there insisting that they must go!

'Essie and Peter must stay,' Nellie said decisively. 'Essie went yesterday with Esther, so there is no need for her to go again, and Peter can go one day next week – now stay like good chickens and play together nicely. Martha is going to make scones and gingerbread, and you could help her.'

'I don't want to make scones and dinger-bread,' said Essie, 'I want to go and see Meg.' She jumped as she spoke, and Bunty, standing in the boat, had to catch her.

'Don't be naughty, Essie,' said Nell. 'Look, your pinafore is all wet, and Peter's boots are wet – neither of you could come like that. Be good and run back with Peter. Put her out again, Bunty.'

The little witch clung to Bunty.

'Dear Bunty, kind Bunty, I can go, can't I? I want to oar – nobody lets me go in boats, nobody lets me oar.' The tears welled up.

'She wouldn't make any difference in the weight, Nell,' said Bunty, vanquished, 'she's only a feather.'

'Only a fefer,' Essie repeated, looking agitatedly at Nell.

'And then poor old Jumbo would be left alone,' Nell said. 'You wouldn't be so selfish, would you, Essie?'

Essie was torn with conflicting emotions – there was Peter standing desolate on the bank, but on the other hand just across the river and down a little way was Meg.

'Oh,' she said, and burst into tears, 'I do want to yock the little baby again.'

'But you were rocking him yesterday, Esther said so,' said Nellie. 'Meg let you have him for a long time.'

'I want him again,' wept Essie. 'I want to schtroke his little teenty feet.'

But clearly someone had to stay. Pip, who was an authority, had said the dinghy could not safely hold more than three. Bunty must go to 'oar' them; Poppet must go, she had not been for a fortnight, having been shut in the house with a cough; and she herself, Nellie, oh she had countless things to consult Meg upon. Peter was making very little outcry at being left; he had said at first disappointedly that he 'wanted to see the kid', but now he stood on the bank quite resigned.

'Put her out, Bunty,' whispered Nell, and Bunty hopped on shore, his young sister clinging tightly to him.

'Hang on to her, Jum,' he said, and Peter manfully pulled at Essie's waist while his elder brother disentangled himself from her frantic hands. The next second Bunty was on board again, and the gay little *Possum* was twenty yards away.

'Go back to the house,' cried Nellie, 'run at once. Peter, take her back, I want to see you inside the white gate.'

For the first few yards Peter had to drag his sister, but after that he evidently told her something consoling, for her sobs ceased, and the boatload saw the little pair walk hand-in-hand up through the rank grass, and disappear within the wicket-gate.

'What a good little fellow Peter is,' Nell said admiringly, and spread the rug comfortably over her knees and Poppet's. 'Now pull away, Bunty, it must be half-past three.'

'I don't think much of you, Nell, dolling up like this,' Bunty said, plying his oars a little viciously. 'If I were Meg I wouldn't like it.'

'What nonsense you talk,' Nell said indignantly. 'Meg knows I have to get dresses sometimes, and I may as well get pretty ones. It wouldn't do her any good for me to get blacks or plain browns.'

'I don't care – it looks like showing off; you could go to her in an old one, and keep these flaring ones for rich people,' persisted the boy.

'I thought you needn't have come in your new hat,' said Poppet. 'Poor Meg, she hasn't had a new hat for a dreadful time.'

Nellie looked fit to cry. 'I always like to ask Meg's opinion of my clothes,' she said, 'you know I wouldn't be so horrid, John. And it isn't a bit an expensive dress.'

'It oughtn't to be, it's so precious ugly,' John said. 'You've as much taste as Flibberty-Gibbet, Nell. There's your dress puce – '

'Puce!' cried Nellie. 'Why it's the loveliest shade of deep Parma violet!'

'Puce,' persisted Bunty, 'and then you go and put red and purple all over your hat.'

'Shows how much you know of colours,' said Nellie; 'that velvet is a lovely shade, just the pinky tinge that helps to make up heliotrope; and the purple is just a richer tone than the dress – I selected them most carefully, and I trimmed it myself.'

'I believe you,' said Bunty, showing his teeth in a grin. 'I suppose you put it in the bottom knob of the banisters and went upstairs and dropped the trimming down on it anyway.'

'Oh,' said Nell, 'I just dropped my bag of ribbons on it, and then stitched on all that clung to it. But it wants something else as a finish, an aigrette or something, that's why I wanted to consult Meg.'

'Look here,' said Bunty, 'if you put another thing on it, I'll give some kids a penny to throw bricks at it. Doesn't it look, Poppet, as if she'd put everything she's got on it?'

But Poppet's eye was a feminine one. 'I think it's lovely,' she said, 'only I wish Meg had one too.'

An hour's row took them across a long slant to the other bank of the river. They tied the boat to a pile of the small rough wharf that was anyone's property now a big important one had been built to meet the wants of this rapidly-growing suburb of Redbank. Down here, near the water, handsome houses nestled in extensive grounds, and the beautiful river frontage was held by the rich, as the bathing and boat houses all along testified.

It was not there that the three stopped; they made their way up, up the River Hill to streets where quiet, modest cottages stood in small, neat allotments of land. One, a tiny pretty place, was running over with roses – they rioted over the fence, up the verandah pillars, peeped gaily into all windows.

Poppet stopped one little second at its gate and sighed. 'If only Megsie lived *here*,' she said.

They went on again – into the business street of the suburb now. It was a dusty, unbeautiful street, built upon thickly on either side. Not a peep of the laughing river could be seen from here, not a tree tossed its free branches in all the length of it, hardly a blade of grass dare show. The Bank was here, the Post Office, the stucco Town Hall of the district, two or three grocers, bootmakers, drapers, all the shops a spreading civilization brings.

Half way down it on one side a terrace stood, a terrace of tall, narrow, commonplace houses, and the middle one bore a brass plate, highly polished, with the name Dr Courtney upon it. Bunty rang the bell, Poppet gazed expectantly at the ugly, maple-grained door in front of her, Nellie looked across the road with pained eyes – across to where the rival butchers of the district, separated only by the circulating library and a confectioner's, tried to cut each other's throats with the tickets on their mutton and beef. To eyes accustomed to the river's witcheries, the thousand greens of the trees, and the free skies round Misrule, the view of hanging carcasses and fly-spotted walls came unpleasantly. A very young maid came to the door, but her cap and apron left nothing to be desired. She beamed at the three, as they passed into the narrow hall. At the sound of their voices Alan came out of his empty consulting room.

He looked ten years older than the day, three years ago, when he led Meg light-heartedly from a rose-strewn altar, in front of Nellie, Poppet, Essie and his own little sister all in fluttering bridesmaids' array. His face was sharper, thinner than the boy Alan's had been, and the always resolute mouth-lines were more pronounced. But the eyes looked out at you quite cheerfully.

'That you, young ones?' he said, pleasure on his face. 'I'm glad you've come, it'll do Meg good to see you. Go straight up – she's trying to make a silk purse out of a sow's ear as usual – you can hear her hammer.'

Nellie looked round.

'You are much straighter than I expected you would be,' she said. 'You know Poppet and I have not seen the house yet, though you have been here a fortnight.'

'Ten days,' he said. 'Does it strike you as a very wretched hole?' His eyes looked round anxiously.

'Oh,' Nell faltered, 'it – it might be worse, Alan.'

'Meg doesn't care a dump, I bet,' Bunty said, with a gruffness that betrayed his sympathy.

Poppet rubbed her cheek against Alan's arm. 'She won't care where she is now she's got little Baby,' she said.

The anxiety died out of the young doctor's face, and he went back to the work he was doing in the consulting room quite cheerfully.

Upstairs the three rushed, and found Meg mounted on steps, putting up curtains of a sunshiny yellow. She sprang down with a glad little cry when the door opened.

'Oh, I *am* glad,' she said. 'Nell, I thought you never were coming – Poppet, you darling – oh, more than one kiss, I haven't seen you for ages. Bunty, I've wanted you a dozen times since last you came – that shelf came down, we couldn't have put strong enough supports, and I have been dying to get on with the other dressing-table.'

Bunty took off his coat in a most business-like fashion, and rolled up his sleeves.

'But where's the nipper?' he said. 'We'll just have a look at him before we start.'

They trooped into an adjacent bedroom, and found Meg's baby on the bed waving its aimless little legs and arms in the air.

'Why, he's awake, the darling darling,' said Nellie, and stooped over him to gather him up in her arms, the new look of tenderness making her face exquisite to see.

Poppet was caressing the warm, wee feet from which she had pulled the boots, putting her finger to be grasped by the fluttering, tiny hand, stroking the downy head.

'Why,' she said, 'oh, Meg, I'm *sure* his eyelashes have grown. Did you cut them? Florrie at our school – you know Florrie, with lovely goldy curls and long eyelashes – well, she said the reason her lashes are so long is that her mother cut them when she was a baby.'

'But they are as long as they can be, without cutting,' Meg said proudly. 'Mrs Lindsay said, Nell, she never saw such long black lashes on so young a child. When I was on the boat yesterday there were quite six babies there, and not one of them had such lovely ones as Little Boy.'

'And I'm sure they hadn't such sweet little mouths,' Poppet said stoutly.

'No, truly they hadn't,' Meg said eagerly, 'they just seemed to have plain, ordinary lips – none of them had a tiny little red bud of a mouth like Baby's.'

'Had they more hair?' said Poppet anxiously.

'Yes, one or two had,' Meg admitted, 'you see, I am not blinded, though I am a mother. I remember, Nell, I was a little disappointed that Baby hadn't a lot of golden curls when he came. But now I wouldn't change for worlds, they couldn't be half so sweet as this soft, brown, downy silk, could they?' And she put her lips down on the dear little head. 'Those babies on the boat who had a lot looked so ordinary. And I must say Little Boy's complexion put all of them in the shade; they were pasty-looking babies, and Boy was so rosy and fresh and smiling everyone was looking at him.'

'Hello, Currant-Eye,' said Bunty. 'Hi, there, look at me – hi, hi, over here, you little donkey, you.' He was waving his arms wildly and contorting his face, and now stooping below the bed foot, and now springing up.

Little Boy continued to gaze calmly and serenely up at the top of the bed.

'Oh, he doesn't quite understand that sort of thing, Bunty,' Meg said apologetically.

'Why, Meg,' said Poppet indignantly, 'you have no eyes – he smiled distinctly. Do it again, Bunty.'

Bunty contorted his body violently again, and said 'Hi, there' and 'Hullo' and 'Here we are again'.

And Baby, gazing about the room, blinked a moment, and shut and opened his hungry little mouth.

'There,' said Poppet triumphantly, 'didn't I tell you – the darlingest little smile, wasn't it, Nell?'

'It certainly was,' Nell said. 'He really is astonishingly knowing for two months, Meg.'

'Yes, I'm afraid he is,' Meg said anxiously, 'sometimes it frightens me a little. My book says babies with too active brains do not thrive as well as duller children. Please don't do it again, Bunty. And I think I'll put him to sleep if you'll all go out for a few minutes; this is too much excitement for him.'

They all went obediently into the next room to await her leisure.

CHAPTER TWO

The Clouds That Came

'Sail on nor fear to breast the sea,
Our hearts, our hopes are all with thee.
Our hearts, our hopes, our prayers, our tears,
Our faith triumphant o'er our fears
Are all with thee – are all with thee.'

This house in Burton's Terrace had only seen ten days of Meg's married life.

The first year of it had been passed in as lovely a home as ever a bride need wish to be taken to. The young couple began on six hundred and fifty pounds a year – Alan's private income of three hundred, and three hundred and fifty from his position in a hospital. That pleasant sum gave them a delightful home in the married quarters at the hospital, three well-trained servants who made the domestic wheels run with a smoothness very soothing to Meg after the jars and creaking of Misrule's wheels, pretty frocks, artistic furniture, plenty of margin for holiday trips, and the amusements that so pleasantly sprinkle the even road of life.

To go to 'Meg's' had been the happiest of excursions to one and all at Misrule.

Major Woolcot himself – the lapse of years had at last brought him this advancement – had enjoyed the well-cooked dainty dinners of Meg's excellent cook after the haphazard arrangements at Misrule, Alan's good cigars, the pleasant company the young couple gathered around them. And Esther liked to go, though once or twice she had looked wistful. This bride was beginning her life on ways much softer to the tread than she, just as young, had done. There were no six harum-scarum children here to take to, no battered furniture, no wild grounds where the weeds grew on an unblushing equality with the flowers.

'You are a very lucky girl, Meg, dear,' she said, when first she saw the beautiful home.

And Nellie, beauty-loving Nellie, it was deep happiness for her to bang the much-banged front door of Misrule behind her and go off, bag in hand, for a week in that dainty home. To be wakened at half-past seven – six was Misrule's usual hour – by a smiling maid with a silver tray and cup of chocolate; to breakfast at luxurious half-past eight in the cosy breakfast-room; to go shopping with Meg – to the best shops, and come back laden with delicious trifles Meg had bought for her – a novel hat-pin, a purse, a lace scarf, a photograph-frame, or such.

To help Meg with a lunch party – perhaps a Violet Lunch – and mass the delicate flowers and arrange the violet ribbons, and help paint violets on the menu cards, and touch all that might be touched with the sweet colour.

To go calling in the afternoon, or stay at home and be called upon. To 'dress for dinner', a pleasant vanity very dear to Nell's heart, and afterwards to be borne off by sister and brother-in-law, who well knew her tastes, to dress-circle seats at the most fashionable piece then running.

But 'an end had come of pleasant places'.

Six months after the marriage the failure of a mine that had seemed safer than any bank had suddenly deprived the young doctor of his private income of three hundred, and at the same time stricken so severe a blow at his father's – old Mr Courtney's – fortune as to make it impossible for him to receive any help from that quarter.

Still, three hundred and fifty was quite enough to live upon. Meg curtailed her expenses, kept only a cook and laundress and one young housemaid, gave up the pretty pony and governess-cart that Alan had bought her, and still found life flowed along a smooth and merry stream.

But then there gathered up on that early marriage sky storm-clouds, black as they had never thought to see.

Serious eye-trouble threatened Alan; more than one oculist friend had looked very grave after examining him.

He struggled on from month to month, refusing to believe anything serious could be the matter; the trouble would yield to mild treatment, he persisted. But every month saw the difficulty increase, his eyes began to blur and fail him at moments critical to his patients. There came a day when, his scalpel at work over a delicate operation, he had almost gone a hairbreadth out of his course and lost the life they were trusting him to patch up.

Then he went home and stared this blank ruin that threatened his life squarely in the face, Meg's hand in his. After the first dark hour passed it was Meg who made the move. They would go to Germany, she said. There were men there who often performed the one operation that the oculists here were agreed upon might be successful in this case, though few of them seemed to care or dare to venture to do the thing themselves.

14

The hospital appointment was given up, the pretty home sold, money borrowed, and the young couple fared forth to wrest from the wiser Old World what the New One could not give them.

Letters came to Misrule from an inexpensive *pension* in a suburb out of Heidelberg. The great doctors gave little hope; even they shrank from the exceeding risk of the great operation, from which one rose either completely blind or with full vision. Alan, left alone, they said, would at all events be able to keep some dim sort of sight for the rest of his life.

The months went on, and the shadows fell heavier and heavier. Meg's letters to Misrule grew thinner every mail – her heavy pen refused to fill the pages.

Then came a postscript to one; a new doctor had been found, full of enthusiasm for the operation; she, Meg, trembled now at the thought of it, but Alan was full of eagerness. A week went past, and another half-sheet came. The operation was to be performed in three days.

Under the far skies where the Southern Cross looked down Misrule walked about, and ate and worked with thoughts and hearts away all the time across the cruel thousands of miles.

'Meg, Meg – oh, don't let it be; God, don't let it be,' came bursting softly from Poppet's wet pillow in the little pink and white peaceful bedroom that had been Meg's all her girlhood.

And Nellie, moving away in the darkness, had looked up from the window at the same quiet stars that had seen so often Meg's happy eyes upraised to them, and had whispered passionately, 'Oh, help her, help her – look where she is now, and help her!' There were no other letters for two mails, and Misrule's heart, quickened before by the immediate anxiety, began to beat heavily, wearily again. Then a blotted, wild line or two telling of success, success beyond even the enthusiastic doctor's expectation. And Misrule flung up its cap, and danced and shouted, and found its river lovely once again, and its skies and stars more glorious than ever, and its world full of kindness.

'Let's let the dogs out,' cried Peter, and rushed off to the stables.

'Let's have a picnic in the boats,' said Poppet.

The months danced along now, both in the old world and the new. Time had to be given for the restored eyes to get back their tone again, but who minded anything now? Meg and Alan laughed and frolicked about in sober Germany for all the world like children out of school. Life that has escaped tragedy by a hairbreadth becomes for the time a picnic.

Back they came at last to their own land, and Misrule had work to keep itself from plunging in the harbour and swimming out to meet the unemotional ship, instead of waiting decorously on the wharf.

The pair were absolutely ruined financially. The hospital appointment had long since passed into other hands, and none other was vacant; they were six hundred pounds in debt, for the travelling and such doctoring had been ruinous; and there was a baby of nine weeks to tie Meg's hands.

But they only laughed at things like these, now that the great clouds were gone.

'As long as I can see what I'm fighting,' said Alan, as he got into harness again, 'I rather enjoy the feeling of having to hit out. Only I'd like things to have been soft for you.'

'As long as you can see what you're fighting,' said Meg

stoutly, 'I don't care a straw if things are hard as nails – so long as we can keep a soft cushion for Baby.'

But it hurt Misrule and the Courtneys, and the old friends of the family, to see them struggling. Many advised that they should go still deeper into debt, and start straight away in a good house, entertain, and live generally in the style one expects from a successful doctor.

But that terrible six-hundred-pound debt made them shrink from more; four hundred old Mr Courtney had lent, and was in somewhat straitened circumstances for want of it; two hundred Major Woolcot had advanced, and would be very glad to have back again in those ever-gaping coffers of his.

There could be no question, therefore, of buying a practice. The little money in hand, apart from the hoped-for fees, would have to see them over more than one cold year perhaps. But in that untempting house in that long, monotonous terrace at Redbank a doctor – of a kind – had long lived, and though he had sold his practice when he left, and the buyer had set up in a handsome house on the heights of the hill, still, someone starting in the same place might gather perhaps a trifle of practice from the association.

They bought nothing but the absolutely necessary articles of furniture for the rooms – just some plain equipments for the consulting room, and chairs, tables and beds for their own use.

'There's the first note of the battle,' Alan said, when, the second day after their arrival, the clang of tools reached them to tell that the highly polished brass plate was being fastened to the front door.

'Hasn't it got a triumphant sound?' Meg answered.

CHAPTER THREE

A Doctrine of Colour

'Well, and if none of these good things came,
What did the failure prove?'

Something seemed sticking in Nell's throat this afternoon as she looked round the brave little home Meg had already contrived, and noticed the lack of even the most ordinary necessities. The front upstairs room was half drawing-room, half study.

'You see people may call,' Meg said gravely, 'so I have had to sacrifice some conveniences to convenances. I could have had it shabbier and more comfortable if I had been certain no one would come.'

'It looks very comfortable,' Nellie faltered, and fell to praising some bookshelves Alan had made.

The velvet carpet of the first drawing-room was only a memory now; this floor was merely painted a dull shade of green, and varnished as Meg had often seen the floors in Denmark and Germany. A rug or two took off the chilly effect. There were a few comfortable rattan chairs, a little

18

table or two, and the other furnishings of the room were books and photographs and some of Misrule's royalty of flowers.

In the bedrooms it was the same; of ordinary furniture there was absolutely nothing but the bedsteads. Packing cases, concealed beneath pretty frilled covers, answered the purposes of dressing-tables, washstands, clothes-cupboards.

The dining room was in the basement, so cheerless a place on first view that even Meg's spirits had received a check. But that floor she painted dull red, and put some bold gleams of colour about, and with a picture or two, a bowl of warm-coloured chrysanthemums, photographs and oddments, the effect was no longer depressing.

'Colour *is* so much, isn't it?' she said, noting Nellie's eye that only looked at the things it might approve of, and seemed not to see the spaces where furniture should be. 'And the drabber life promises to be the more we want of it. I'm sure our mutton-chops taste better with those bits of red and gold and blue to catch our eyes when we look up from our plates.'

'I'm quite sure they do,' Nell said. 'I think it was sweet of you to think of it, Meg. Some girls would have been so miserable at seeing all their pretty things sold, they would not have troubled like you have done.'

'Oh,' said Meg, 'that sort of thing has become quite a creed with me. Some day I shall go into the high-ways – meaning by that all the most depressing, wretched little streets I can find – and preach a doctrine of colour to the women and girls.'

'They would only apply it to their hats,' said Pip, who

had just come in and bestowed a greeting kiss on the top of Meg's fair head.

'Poor things,' Meg said, 'I never condemn the most dreadful hats I see on public holidays. I always feel there must be such a terrible amount of grey and drab in the background of the picture to have induced the little burst of brilliance. But I should tackle the middle-aged women chiefly with my colour scheme, and the young mothers – more especially the young mothers.'

'I'll come with you and preach some saving clauses about cleanliness,' laughed Pip. 'Your women would run riot, carried away by your ideas, and rush home and hang red art muslin over the dirty patches on the wall that need a scrubbing-brush more than anything.'

'Well, perhaps I'll take you with me,' Meg said, 'there might be that danger. I do know I'd rather bring brightness and cleanliness into the dun-coloured homes of our own country, than undertake the most promising mission to the heathen Chinee.'

Pip pushed a chair forward. 'Up you get,' he said, 'the orator is worthy of his stump. I suppose the infant is the cause of all this eloquence?'

Meg laughed and sat down comfortably on the proffered stump. 'Forgive me,' she said, 'yes, I suppose it *is* Baby. Some way when you have children you get a feeling of an odd sort of responsibility for the poor old world. What *have* you got there, Youth?'

Pip was taking the wrappings off a brightly coloured picture book, a Noah's Ark, and a little horse on wheels.

'For the kid,' he said. 'I saw them in a window as I came along, and thought the little chap could amuse himself with them when you were busy.'

A tear sprang to Meg's eye, though her mouth worked with a laugh. Pip was serving his articles in a solicitor's office, and had the smallest of salaries in the meantime, yet he had never yet paid her a visit without bringing 'something for the kid'.

His first gift, sent when perhaps the child was six weeks old, was a box of soldiers and a tin train.

'But you dear, ridiculous old fellow,' Meg said, 'Little Boy could as easily play with the moon as these things. You mustn't waste your money on him till he is older and gets a spine and thumbs. He can't even pick anything up yet.'

'Oh,' said Pip, 'you give him the chance. I bet you he'll start to pull the horse about as soon as he sees it, and stand the animals in twos. Well, I'll go down and have a smoke with Alan, I told him I'd be back in a second.'

But before he could turn away the door opened, and there entered two dripping wet atoms, Peter, with Essie held by the hand, and Alan behind.

'What on earth!' began Meg, with startled eyes.

Peter and Essie only looked at each other and giggled.

'Peter!' cried Meg. 'Essie! What is the matter, what have you been doing?'

'Peter!' cried Nellie. 'Essie! Oh, I will never trust you again, never.'

'I told Lizzie to light the water-heater,' Alan said. 'Get their clothes off, Meg, and see what's happened when they've had a hot bath and a drink.'

The story, however, came out during the process.

Bunty was building a canoe in the Misrule boat shed; true, it was not by any means finished, and he would have thought twice before he had gone a hundred yards in it himself at its present stage, but in this craft the two children had actually voyaged across the river. The current had been favourable, and Peter had been able to make a certain amount of way with the short paddle, but the passage took some time.

'We were as right as rain,' said Peter, 'and we'd got right up to that white wharf, the one before this one, and then what must that little idiot Essie do but tip out into the water.'

Essie buried her nose in Meg's shoulder.

'I was just letting Mussie put her footies in the water, and I let go of her,' she whispered.

And the excuse had to be taken. 'Mussie' was a purple and pink cow, perhaps four inches long, that the child had kept and loved devotedly since she was three. She took it to bed with her, it was in her pocket in school hours, it stood patiently beside her plate at every meal. There had even been a Sunday when Nellie, looking up at church from her prayers to shake her head at Peter, who was giggling audibly, had been forced to smile herself, for there was Mussie on a spare hassock beside little kneeling Essie, Mussie reared up in a devotional attitude, with his purple head resting piously on an opened prayer book.

And Mussie, being lost overboard, what wonder the distracted Essie leaned recklessly over the side, and finally 'tipped out'?

Peter, a ridiculous object, with Baby's shawl around him, was having his head well scrubbed with a bath towel.

'Of course I had to get in after the young idiot,' he said.

'You neederent,' said Essie, 'I can swim's well as you.'

'Well, you squealed hard enough,' Peter said.

'My newest frock was getting wet,' said Essie, with dignity.

Peter giggled. 'Wasn't it a lark with the gentleman?' he said.

Essie giggled. 'As if we'd get drownded when we was close to the wharf like that.'

It seemed a gentleman, who had been smoking in one of the gardens that ran down to the water, had heard Essie's first shriek and had rushed headlong down to their assistance. When he arrived on the wharf, however, both the children had swum to the side, and he had nothing to do but give them a hand up. Their presence of mind and excellent swimming impressed him, however; when they refused to come up to the house and be dried, alleging that they could run to their sister's as quickly, he put his hand in his pocket and brought out a sovereign for each of them.

'That's because you've learnt to swim,' he said. 'You have really saved me a great deal of trouble. I should have felt obliged to jump in after you, and then rub you both to life again if you hadn't swum in so well.'

Nothing could show the children the wrongfulness of their act. They kept gazing at their gold with lustrous eyes; in all their lives before they had never been presented with anything of greater value than half-a-crown.

'We can get our tricycles now,' Peter chuckled, 'and we've waited a simply awful time for them.'

Essie's thoughts traversed back, too, over the months they had longed ardently for these things.

'What a pity we never tipped over before,' she said regretfully.

CHAPTER FOUR

Misrule on Wheels

Pip's was the first bicycle in the family, and Major Woolcot had never grudged the twenty pounds he paid for it.

For as he grew to man's estate Pip seemed to forget the stable had been built and stocked expressly for his father's benefit. He had a genial way of saddling Mazeppa or Mopoke and going off for a long ride early on Sunday morning, returning at dinner-time, flushed with the exercise, and saying, 'You really ought to have gone out, governor – it was a perfect morning.'

'I should have gone,' the Major would return coldly, 'only you had taken Mopoke.'

And the next week Pip would take Mazeppa, and then it would fall out that the Major had intended to use that steed. Moreover, all the time the boy was out the Major would fume and fret about the place. He knew how it would be – the young beggar would bring the poor brute home lame. He knew what it would be – Mopoke would be in a lather when she came back, and would get another chill. He knew what it would be – that boy would force Mazeppa at a fence he could not take, and would bring him back with broken knees. None of these things ever happened, but the Major was prepared for them every week, and Esther and the household were the sufferers for every ride.

Then Alan invested in a bicycle for his rounds, being quite unable to keep a horse and buggy. And Andrew followed suit, and Pip learned to ride his machine and occasionally borrowed it.

'By Jove,' he said one day, when he and his father were looking at the horses, 'Mopoke's eating her head off; I'll have to take it out of her on Sunday.'

'She's all right,' said his father jealously. 'I don't want her ridden to death. Work off your spirits on that bicycle you were trying the other day.'

'It's Andrew Courtney's,' Pip said gloomily. 'He's going off on a tour with some other fellows. Lucky dog!'

The Major looked at him narrowly. 'You don't mean to tell me you'd rather ride a bicycle than a horse?' he said.

'Wouldn't I, though!' said Pip, who had been used to horses always, and was full of the newer craze.

The Major could hardly credit his ears. 'You mean to say if you had a bicycle of your own you wouldn't want to use my horses?' he said.

'Not I,' said Pip, scenting a victory he had never thought of fighting for. 'If I could have afforded a bike when Andrew got his, Mopoke wouldn't have felt my weight at all these Sundays that she has done.'

'How much are these bicycles?' said the Major cautiously.

Pip flicked at a fly that was haunting Mazeppa's nose. 'Andy gave twenty-five pounds for his,' he said, 'but that's rather stiff. Alan's was twelve pounds, but his tyres were a good way from new. Still, it's easy to pick up a good second-hand one if you know your way about.'

. The Major rubbed Mopoke's pleasant nose thoughtfully. Of late the worry he had felt about Pip riding his horses had almost determined him to buy him a mount of his own. He would never realise that this son of his was grown up and beyond his school-boy tricks; indeed, he never got over an uneasy feeling that if left unwatched his eldest son might 'shy a cricket ball' and lame a horse, as Bunty had done on one memorable occasion.

He had even, with an eye to providing the boy with something that would keep him off the backs of Mopoke and Mazeppa, looked at a horse a brother officer wanted to sell for twenty pounds. But then the stables would need enlarging, and the feed bill was already a very serious one. Pip's bicycle enthusiasm seemed a marvellous solving of the problem.

'Are you sure you wouldn't be tired of it in a week and want to go back to the horses?' he said. He had a curious contempt and distrust for bicycles himself.

'Tired of it!' said Pip. 'You just try me.'

So the Major handed over a cheque for twenty pounds, and Pip haunted all the bicycle shops in town, and brought home piles of catalogues, and was heard to speak of nothing for a fortnight but gears and sprockets and tyres, free-wheels and chainless machines. Finally a selection was made – a glittering Swallow came home to Misrule, and one person in the world was perfectly happy.

Then Bunty caught the fever.

Pip was not particularly selfish, but it was too severe a strain on his patience to see a young brother clumsily handling his tenderly-cared-for machine, and making wild essays to ride it round the paths.

High words were heard several times between them, Pip having discovered almost invisible scratches on the enamel or the nickel, and Bunty contending that they were far more likely caused by Pip, who had ridden it forty miles the day before, than he, Bunty, who had merely taken a turn round the lawn.

'And smashed into a fence once and a tree twice on the way,' Pip would say scathingly. 'Look at the handle-bars; they're twisted, I'm certain.'

One morning as his father was just riding off to barracks, Bunty touched his elbow and presented a sheet of paper. On it was a column of careful figures. The first entry had to do with the enormous and extortionate charge of the quarterly boat ticket, and the additional tram fares necessited by the distance between Misrule and the college where Bunty was supposed to be preparing for the University.

The document, to be precise, ran as follows:

Moneys obtained by extortion from Major Woolcot for the school travelling of his son John –

To one quarter's boat ticket by the slow old river tub which wastes no end of valuable time that should be given to Euclid and the classics .... £1   19s.   0d.

(And it'll be more soon, for I can't get a school ticket when I start to the University.)

To one quarter's tram tickets .... 13s. 0d.

(And this may be much more any day, for the tram is so crowded I always have to hang on to the platform, and so make you run the risk of paying a doctor's bill for me.)

Total drain for the quarter on Major Woolcot's pocket, exclusive of risks................................ £2 12s. 0d.

Or for five years the enormous sum of........ £52 0s. 0d.

AGAINST THIS

Set the following facts

Down at Hewett's, the bicycle mender's, there's a first-rate little machine going for the ridiculous sum of ..... £9 0s. 0d.

Thus in five years, after the one outlay, the sum left over in Major Woolcot's pocket for investment at 7 per cent (if he can get it) will be .... £43 0s. 0d.

ADVANTAGES

Splendid, healthy exercise every day, instead of being mewed up in a dirty old boat and a stuffy tram.
(N.B. – Giles, our drill sergeant, says I need more exercise.)

Machine always at hand if you want a message taken into Sydney, or Esther needs anything in a hurry from the grocer's, or the children are taken dangerously ill in the night.

The document departed in its last line from its business-like character. It said, 'Go on, pater' and the very black writing of the three words gave them such an urgent look that the Major 'went on'.

Bunty, coming home for tea that same evening, found on his plate an envelope in his father's writing.

He tore it open, trembling, and a cheque for nine pounds burnt his hand and made his head swim. On the envelope flap was written, 'With thanks for your unusual and considerate interest in my expenditure, J. Woolcot – P.S. Get Pip or someone to go and have a look at it'.

Pip went, distrustful of such a price – but saw and was conquered. 'A remarkably good little machine for the money, and very little used,' was his verdict, and Bunty tossed on his narrow bed all night, and could hardly wait for Saturday's dawn to come and set him free to rush down to the shop, cheque in hand, and wrest the machine from the man's possession.

Martha gave him a plate of porridge and some toast in the kitchen, seeing he would not hear of waiting until orthodox breakfast-time.

'But look you here,' she said, 'and be warned in time – if you go and take my tea-towels and glass-cloths to clean the nasty dirty thing like Mr Philip does, I'll smash it with the axe, or my name's not Martha Tomlinson.'

(Poor Martha, it was, alas, that name still; Malcolm, in honest desire to alter it, had even gone off to Western Australia to see what might be done there, but fate was against him, and he was back in Sydney again waiting with Micawber-like cheerfulness for something to turn up.)

Bunty was quite willing to promise. 'Anything will do for me,' he said, 'your afternoon aprons, or a nice soft blouse – I'm not particular, bless your soul!'

'And just let me see you setting your greasy oil-can down

on my clean dresser like Mr Philip did – just let me see it, that's all,' cautioned Martha.

'Just let me see you using my bottle of oil for your old salad dressings, that's all,' said Bunty.

'And boiling his dirty old keroseny chain in the little milk-saucepan, the new enamel double saucepan. "An' it'll wash, keep your hair on," sez he. And didn't I scrub and scour with sandstone and carbolic for a week, and then the first time I put the milk in again didn't the master tear and rage round the table and ask had I emptied a lamp over the porridge? An' isn't it standing there in the scullery still, no good to no one?'

'That's a throw in,' said Bunty. 'I shall want something to boil *my* chain in.'

Then Poppet came bursting in, struggling with the buttoning behind of her clean holland frock as she came. Of course she was to go with Bunty to 'help choose', but equally of course he had appropriated first bath and she had been unable to catch up till now.

'Late as usual,' he said, buttering himself a fresh slice of toast; 'never saw such things as girls. Here, come here, what are you trying to do – does it go in this button? Well, stand still. There, see what you've made me do now.'

He had reached carelessly over the table to get at the buttoning, and his cup of cocoa went to make a flood on the clean kitchen table.

Martha, always somewhat

> 'Surly through getting up early!
> And tempers are short in the morning,'

came down upon them heavily. 'Two breakfasts being got

ready, one in the nurs'ry and one in the breakfast-room, and here two of you come worriting me for another. No, you can just clear out of this, Miss Poppet; I'm not going to have you dirtying up my table, you can just wait till the proper time.'

'Oh, Martha, dear Martha – just a scrap of porridge – I *must* go with Bunty,' entreated Poppet.

'Not a scrap,' said Martha, 'serve you both just right to have to wait – look at that table.'

Bridget, filling the hot-water cans, proffered consolation.

'Why, the shop won't be open, Master John,' she said. 'Why can't you both wait and have your breakfastses comfortable, and go off quietly after?'

'And let another fellow get there first and take my machine! I see myself,' said Bunty. 'Once people get a scent of what a bargain it is the traffic will be stopped with every one rushing to buy it.'

'Faith, it's my experience there's always a better bargain still round the corner,' said Bridget, departing with her cans, for Pip's voice could be heard from the stair-top demanding his shaving-water.

'What's Malcolm doing down at the stables as early as this?' said Bunty.

'Malcolm!' cried the amazed Martha. 'Why, he was to have gone to that new place this morning – what can it mean?'

She put down the bacon she was cutting, and knife in hand stalked off to demand of her lover why he was missing another chance.

'Here, you'll have to look sharp – where's a plate?' said Bunty. 'Is that enough, or can you eat more?'

'Heaps,' said Poppet, and seized the plateful of porridge

he had ladled from the saucepan on the stove, poured milk upon it, and swallowed it in choking haste.

'Take a drink.' Bunty proffered an enamelled mug, and Poppet drank a scalding mouthful or two. 'We can eat our toast as we go – come on – we'd better cut at once. Here she is coming back, and she'll want to throw the saucepans at us.'

CHAPTER FIVE

A Bicycle Built for Two

They were at the bicycle shop exactly an hour before the man opened it and prepared for the custom of the day. Perhaps, had he known there was a nine-pound cheque burning a would-be customer's pocket just outside, he might have hastened himself a little more.

The boy and girl employed the interval in looking through the glass window, which fortunately had no blind, and examining the various machines standing within. To Bunty's intense relief his marvellous bargain, the Fleetfoot, stood just in the same spot it had stood in for the past month, and its fly-spotted price card still hung to its handle-bars.

'I've been in no end of a funk all night thinking someone might have gone in after Pip,' he said. 'There was a fellow there when I was in yesterday afternoon, and he looked at it several times.'

33

'But you could have had one of the others,' consoled Poppet. 'Look, there's one in that corner, only eight pounds, and it's a much prettier colour. Why didn't you choose a nice red one, Bunty, instead of that plain black?'

'Just like a girl,' said Bunty. 'You'd buy it for its colour, and never look to see if anything else was right. That one happens to have worn-out tyres, and is very low gear. Just look at my little beauty beside it – there's as much difference as between an elephant and a swan.'

'Oh,' said Poppet, pressing her nose very close against the glass, 'wouldn't *I* love one! Fancy going flying down Red Hill with your feet up like Pip does. O-o-o-oh, *wouldn't* it be lovely! That little red one up in the corner, yes, that would just do for me. And when you went out I could come too, and we could race everywhere.'

'You!' said Bunty. 'You're too young, of course. And you wouldn't be game to get on one. It's not as easy as it looks.'

'It's pretty easy,' said Poppet.

'Why, you've never tried in your life,' cried Bunty.

Poppet had the grace to blush somewhat. 'You needn't say anything about it,' she said, and looked carefully round as if to make quite sure her eldest brother was not within earshot, 'but once or twice when Pip's left his at home, and no one's been about anywhere, I've had a go on it.'

'Then it must have been *you* who made those scratches,' said Bunty, gazing at her.

'No,' said Poppet, 'because I looked 'ticularly every time it fell to see if I had hurt it, but I was on the grass, and there's nothing to scratch it there.'

'And you mean to say you actually got on to the thing!' ejaculated Bunty, staring at her with new eyes.

'Oh,' said Poppet modestly, 'I had to try a good many

times first. I kept mounting from the garden seat – it's a lot easier than getting up like you do.'

'But you mean to say you stuck on it?' cried Bunty.

Poppet was nothing if not strictly honest. 'I fell off a lot of times first,' she said, 'and I got a lot of bruises, but the third day I went twice round the grass near the stables. I'd have gone three times only I kept looking up at the house to see if Pip was home, and it made me tip over.'

Bunty gazed at her admiringly; more than this he could not manage himself. Then he looked through the window and viewed the little red machine.

'Perhaps,' he said hopefully, 'you could write a letter to the pater like I did, and he might get you one.'

But Poppet shook her head sadly. 'What could I say it would save?' she said. 'I only go to school in the nursery. Oh, no, I'll never get one, of course – I'm not thinking of it, only sometimes when you see anyone go spinning past with their feet up, you feel as if your breath goes, you want it so.'

Here the man opened the door and Bunty cannonaded inside, and rushed up to feel that the Fleetfoot was actually steel and india-rubber, and not a delightful but unsubstantial dream. The man did not take very much notice of him beyond wishing him a cheerful good morning – the boy had hung about the place for over a month on his way to school, each day gazing with loving eyes at the nine-pound machine – he was not to know this particular day was marked bright red in the calendar.

'Not gone yet?' said Bunty, playing with his pleasure a moment before he grasped it altogether.

'No, not yet,' said the man, 'but there was a gentleman looking at it hard last night.'

Bunty's startled hand dived at once into his pocket for the cheque.

'Won't the little girl hurt herself?' the man said. 'Oh, I beg your pardon, I can see she's used to them.'

Bunty followed his gaze and found Poppet engaged in mounting one after the other the nine or ten second-hand ladies' machines that stood awaiting customers. She had looked across and seen Bunty and the man talking – such an opportunity, she told herself, might never occur again – since Bunty was spending here nine wonderful pounds, the man could hardly object to her trying the mounting of these easy machines that had no difficult bar like Pip's. Up she jumped into saddle after saddle, settling herself, pretending to be riding away out of the fixtures, sitting with her arms folded, putting her small feet up for an imaginary but very lovely coast.

How her cheeks glowed – how her eyes danced! It might have been Judy herself who sat on the little saddles and looked challengingly out on the world.

The man sauntered up to her. 'What machine do you ride, miss?' he said.

'Me!' cried Poppet. 'Why, I haven't one, of course.'

'Then you ought to have,' said the man. 'I can see you have a natural aptitude for it, the way you jump on. Why don't you get your pa to buy you one? That one you're on, it's a bit knocked about p'raps, but all of it's there, and it won't fall to pieces. I got it a bargain, and I'd let it go for four pounds.'

Four pounds! He might just as well have said forty. Poppet hardly listened to him, being occupied now in noticing a machine that had a free-wheel attached.

'Four pounds!' breathed Bunty, and came over to it, and stood and gazed at it with strange eyes.

'See for yourself, you seem to have an eye for machinery – look at it well yourself and tell me if it's not worth the money.'

Bunty went down on his knees; he asked for a wrench and unscrewed the cranks, and took the saddle off, and tapped at all the enamelled parts to find a crack, and even took off the chain-guard that he might test the chain.

'You persuade your pa to let her have it,' the man said; 'an eager young lady like her ought to have a chance.'

Bunty breathed hard as he stood up; his face was pale, his eyes gleamed a little. He dragged the man to the other end of the shop.

'Have you got any others – men's, I mean – cheaper than the nine-pound one?' he said.

'Yes, I've got them from five pounds up,' the man said.

'But it would have to be a really decent one,' said Bunty, for he felt he owed it in honour to his father to buy one that would carry him five years at least.

'Here's a good make, a bit battered, of course, but it's well worth its price – six pounds,' the man said. 'Here's another – only came in yesterday, seven pounds – knocked about a bit, but not at all bad. Still, that one you seem to fancy, the Fleetfoot, is worth more than the two pounds extra.'

Bunty wiped the sweat off his forehead with his coat-sleeve. 'Give me that wrench again,' he said, and his voice sounded a trifle hoarse. He was half-an-hour kneeling by the seven-pound machine, testing it, unscrewing various parts; he even took out the ball-bearings, examined them, and put them back. He stood all the time with his back carefully turned to the Fleetfoot.

Poppet grew impatient. 'You'll have no time to try it today if you're so long,' she urged. 'Come on – 'tisn't as if you don't know which to take – you said you wouldn't have any in the world but the Fleetfoot.'

Bunty stood up and looked away from her.

'This one is a very good one too,' he said, 'it's as sound as anything. I'm going to have this.'

'But it's only seven pounds,' said Poppet.

'Why ever shouldn't you spend all the cheque? He gave you nine and didn't tell you to save any.'

'We're going to get two machines,' said Bunty, 'that red one you were on for you and this fellow for me. The man says we can owe him the other two pounds for six months – only, of course, we'll both have to stump up our pocket money every week, all that time, till it's paid.'

'Bunty!' almost screamed Poppet. She flew across the room to the red machine that Bunty had tested so carefully; she touched it to make sure it was real; she flew back to Bunty.

'Oh, you're in fun – of course you're only in fun,' she said. 'It couldn't really happen that *I* should have one.' A painful scarlet stood in her cheeks.

Bunty addressed himself to the man.

'Give me a receipt for the two machines,' he said. 'You can put it at the end that two pounds are left owing.'

'No, no,' said Poppet. She caught at the man's arm as he proceeded to fill in the receipt. 'Only one machine we are taking – I won't let you – we only want the Fleetfoot, please.'

'Hold your tongue,' said Bunty gruffly.

Poppet paid another excited visit to the red machine.

'Oh, it couldn't – it couldn't truly, really be mine,' she said again, 'and oh, oh, I *couldn't* let you give up the Fleet-foot – you wouldn't like the other half so well.'

'It's a jolly good little machine,' said Bunty. 'I'll get to like it no end soon.'

'Would you really – oh, would you *really*?' Poppet said, torn with conflicting desires. '*I* think it's prettier than the Fleetfoot, 'cause it's green, but I never thought you would. Green is a *lovely* colour, I think.'

A lovely colour! Bunty considered its hue so nearly allied to that of his bedstead at home that he was going to spend the only shilling he had in the world on a pot of black enamel to cover it up as speedily as might be.

'Oh yes, it's gay enough,' he said. 'Come on, I haven't a stiver left now I have got this paint, so we'll have to stump it home – can't go in the boat. But it's only four miles, if we go the short cut.'

They went the short cut, which included hills without end, up which they had to drag their bicycles. When they came to flat, lonely stretches they climbed into their saddles and went a few steps, and fell off and bruised themselves, and rose up and mounted again, and fell off again.

They were covered in dust and grime when they finally reached Misrule's gate. Poppet had a torn stocking and had a badly-abraded knee beneath it, an angry lump on her forehead, very little skin on the palms of her hands, and sore places all over her body. Bunty's hat-brim was broken, he had two jagged rents in his coat, and various swollen places on his cheeks and forehead.

But the bicycles were their own, and they had brought them home themselves! At the gate they gave a whoop of triumph that brought the whole family running out on the path. Then, their audience all there and staring, they mounted shakily at the gate, wheeled excited erratic courses down the long drive, and fell into an inextricable collision with each other and a tree near the steps.

Thus had Misrule three bicycles to its credit.

CHAPTER SIX

A Little List

'Two added to one – if that could be done,'
It said, 'with one's fingers and thumbs.'
The Hunting of the Snark

'Oh, Esther, *do* beg him. Oh, I am just longing to have it – I'll never be nineteen again, and that's the most important age of all – up to eighteen you're a child to a certain extent, but at nineteen you are really and truly a woman.'

This from Nellie who, four years ago, had insisted that fifteen was 'grown up'.

'But a dance would be so dreadfully expensive, Nell,' Esther said, 'I am really afraid to think of it. Wouldn't a little tennis-party do? Afternoon tea is a mere nothing, and you could have ices to make it more festive than usual.'

'A tennis-party, and with one court, and the grounds in the state they are!' Nellie looked at Esther reproachfully.

'Well, a moonlight picnic or a gipsy tea to some new place,' begged Esther.

'Oh, Essie, if you *knew* how I'd set my heart on a dance,' said Nellie. 'I'd be as economical afterwards as possible and

41

help you make tons of jam to save the grocer's bill, and help with the sewing instead of getting in Miss Grey. I'll even go without the new dress you said I could have! Oh, *do* beg him to, Esther.'

'I must say I'm frightened at the prospect,' Esther said. 'Just think of the terrible upset and expense there was at Meg's wedding – apart from the frocks it would be nearly as bad. This is a most inconvenient house for entertaining.'

'But we would have it *much* simpler than at the wedding,' pleaded Nell, 'and the boys and Poppet and I would do nearly everything.'

In came the boys and Poppet, and Essie, and the beautiful plans were laid open to their criticisms.

'You go to whips of dances about here,' said Bunty, 'one would think you got enough of it. Let other people pay for them and you go and enjoy them, that's my advice. And spend what it would have cost on that bike at Green's, Nell, – it's a real A-oner.'

'Thank you,' said Nellie, 'but if I ever do get a bicycle, Bunty, I shan't trouble *you* to choose it. Of all battered, disreputable specimens yours and Poppet's are about the worst.'

'Looks aren't everything,' said Bunty, but he flushed a little. The machines were not all the man had painted them or that they had seemed at his own inexperienced examination of them; they were clumsy, heavy things compared with the models of the hour, and took an immense amount of strength to get them over the hills. Also they had given way in several parts, and there being no pocket money available to either owner for six months, they were mended when practicable with string or wire.

'I wouldn't ride any other – mine's just perfection,'

Poppet said warmly, and truly felt so. She had come to have the feeling for the dumb and shabby steel thing that one often gets for a long-used favourite horse.

'I don't know that it isn't about time we did give something, Esther,' Pip said. 'We are always getting invitations to something or other, and it's precious little we give in return.'

This made Esther consider it more carefully; hospitable claims must be fulfilled. You were always welcome to drop into Misrule to tea or dinner, though the chances were you would only get a very plain meal; and picnics were frequent and free; but copy its neighbours and indulge in big 'evenings' and dances this house had never done.

'Think how shabby the furniture is,' said Esther, glancing round.

'At night it never shows – we can do wonders with flowers and draperies,' said Nell eagerly, for Esther's tone showed signs of softening.

'What would be the Mantilinian total?' said Pip. 'I suppose it's the supper that's the great crux.'

'Yes, that's it,' sighed Nell. 'What *do* people want supper for? As long as I had a glass or two of lemonade at a dance I wouldn't care if there was no supper-room at all. The dancing is the great thing.'

'Oh, that's all very well for a girl,' Pip said, 'but a man has to eat to dance, though he may not dance to eat. The older I grow the more necessary I find it to keep two spaces on the programme to myself, and go and have a good plate of beef and salad before I tackle the second half of the programme.'

'That's because you'll never stop being a school-boy,' said Nell, her nose in the air. 'Real men don't think of things like that.' Her thoughts went to a 'real man' who had lately appeared on her horizon.

'Don't you make any mistake,' said Pip, 'when I was a kid I just went for the most bilious-looking trifle and cakes on the table, and gulped them down after I'd finished scrambling for jelly for the girls, and then I'd cut back to the ball-room so as not to keep a partner waiting. I'm wiser now, that's all.'

'If we could get an idea of the cost,' said Esther. 'That was a frightful bill from the caterer after Meg's wedding. Your father almost had a fit. I simply dare not broach the notion to him.'

'We would have everything *most* simple,' said Nell.

'But you must have *enough*,' said Pip.

'Get a sheet of paper, Bunty – you're best at figures,' said Nell. 'Now let's all put our heads together and see how little we can do it for. How much to you think you could get out of him, Esther?'

Esther looked distressed. 'He has just had to pay the butcher's bill – fourteen pounds – for me,' she said. 'I got so badly behind with last quarter's accounts.'

'Whew!' said Pip, 'and then twenty for my bike.'

'And nine pounds to me,' said Bunty. 'I think it will be jolly rough on him if you ask him for a red cent – he's not made of gold.'

Nellie looked miserable.

'If we only have a very little one, Essie, and a *very* simple supper, don't you think you could manage it out of the housekeeping money?' she said.

'Yes, there's something in that,' assented Pip. 'Couldn't you make the things yourselves?'

'You all seem to think that things that can go down on

the grocer's bill cost nothing,' said Esther. 'But let us think what we'll need. Tea, coffee, lemonade – '

'We must have claret cup,' Nell said, 'but that is *very* cheap. Six bottles will make those two art bowls full – you can put such a lot of water and lemons to it.'

'It will be strictly non-intoxicating, made by Nellie's recipe, so I needn't object,' laughed Esther. 'Put down nine shillings for the claret, Bunty – eighteen-pence a bottle is good enough for that.'

Bunty groaned as he wrote down the figures. 'It would pay for a cyclometer and a lamp,' he said.

'Now eatables: sandwiches, cakes, trifles, jellies,' said Nellie. 'That's all.'

'Fruit,' said Bunty.

'Fruit salad,' exclaimed Poppet, 'and let me make it.'

'Fortunately we are getting a good deal of cream at present,' Esther said comfortingly.

'Sweets – we'd have to have little plates of chocolates and things,' said Nellie, 'but I can make date creams and French jellies, so I dare say five shillings would cover that expense.'

'I think you ought to have a joint or two on the sideboard for the men,' said Pip; 'meat's cheap – I'm not even suggesting poultry.'

'Well, I'll give you a big round of corned beef, and a lot of good salad. You can undertake the dressing, Nell – Martha is apt to get it curdled.'

'Let there be enough trifle,' said Bunty. 'I don't want to ask some girl to have some and then go and find it's all gone, like I did at Poppet's party.'

'Fruit,' said Esther. 'There are only apples and pears left in the orchard. Do you think with some bananas and oranges that would do? Very few care for fruit late at night.'

'We can get passionfruit from the Courtneys,' said Nellie, 'there's a fence covered with it, and no one eating them, and we can put them in custard-glasses with whipped cream on top. I'm afraid we can't venture on ices or ice-creams, can we? They're lovely, I always think, and seem to give quite a different tone to a dance. Don't you think we could? It hardly comes to anything yet, does it, Bunty?'

'They are so very dear, and you want such a lot,' said Esther, 'and then there are plates and spoons extra – as it is, I'm afraid we shall have to hire some crockery and glasses. It is very seldom we have more than one dozen unbroken tumblers in the house at one time.'

'Tell you,' said Peter, 'get the man that comes round with the bugle, he gives you an awful lot for a penny – red or yellow or pink in a big egg-cup. Me and Essie – '

'What's this?' demanded Esther. 'Have you been buying from that man again after what I told you? Dirty, unwholesome stuff, made no one knows where!'

'It didn't hurt us,' said Peter consolingly, 'and it isn't a bit dirty, is it, Ess? We only had a ha'penny too between us, so we didn't get much. But I should think for half-a-crown he'd give you all in his cart, and lend you the egg-cups too.'

'I'm afraid even that would be too dear at the price,' laughed Esther. 'No, Nell, we will let ices strictly alone.'

'Very well,' sighed Nellie.

'Add up, cashier,' said Esther.

Bunty figured away.

'Four pounds seven shillings,' he said, 'sheer, downright waste. Why, you could go for a tour down the South Coast, and get a free-wheel put on to your machine into the bargain.'

'Four pounds seven,' said Esther thoughtfully.

Pip felt in his pockets, drew out a handful of money and counted it. 'Three pounds,' he said. 'I'm afraid I'll have to keep one back to keep me going to the end of the quarter. But you can have the other two.'

There was a brief outburst of admiration at his generosity.

'I've only seventeen-and-six left in my allowance,' Nell said, 'but I can put in all that. I'll just manage with my old shoes and gloves, and not waste money on boat-fares and trams.'

Bunty and Poppet looked at each other unhappily; their hands were so tied with their debt.

'If someone will lend me some, and wait to be paid till the bike man's finished with, I could give some of the next half-year's pocket money,' Bunty began.

'No, you've done quite enough; you can stand out of this,' Pip said shortly. He thought more than he said about that bicycle of Poppet's when he remembered it had not even occurred to him to try to save out of his twenty pounds.

Essie gave a joyful skip. 'You can have our pounds that we got for tipping out of the boat,' she said.

Peter added a clause to the generous offer.

'Only then all the supper what's over is ours,' he said.

The family gently rejected this splendid donation, and reminded the offerers about the tricycles that the toy shop still held.

'Two-seventeen-six in hand,' said Bunty.

Nellie blushed a little. 'If you hear father mentioning anything about a birthday present, Esther – he *did* begin to say something about that little, sweet little brooch I'd been looking at in Hardy's – you might – ' she paused.

'Just mention to him that a small cheque would meet with more favour,' finished Esther. 'Very well.'

'Girls are queer cattle,' Bunty said. 'You don't catch *me* offering *my* birthday presents for other people to eat up.'

'Two pounds seventeen-and-six, and a small and only prospective cheque – it isn't very much,' said Esther, 'but I suppose it must be managed. You shall have it, chickens.'

Nellie's eyes were lustrous. 'Now let us think of what dances we'll have,' she said; 'nearly all waltzes and lancers, eh?'

'Oh,' said Poppet ecstatically, 'little programmes and tassels and pencils! Let me give them out.'

Nell's eyes lost their lustre. 'We forgot to count the programmes,' she said in some consternation, 'and the pencils and the cards – oh, dear!'

Esther made another imaginary dip into the allowance her father made her yearly, and that she quietly applied to so many needs besides her own.

'I'll undertake the pencils and cords,' she said, 'and we could buy those gilt-edged correspondence cards, fold them double, and you and Meg could etch or paint some pretty designs on them, Nell.'

Nellie gave her hand a squeeze. 'You always were a brick, Essie,' she said. 'Now, how many shall we ask? With all furniture out and the folding-doors open there's really a lot of room. How many do you think?'

'Thirty?' said Esther. 'Fifteen couples, not counting ourselves?'

'Oh, Esther, that *would* be a few – fifty at least – we might *ask* sixty or seventy, there are sure to be some refusals. Fifty would be just a nice number.'

'Precious little room to dance,' said Bunty. 'I need an awful lot of room myself to turn a girl well round in.'

'Oh, with a garden and a staircase and the verandahs there'll be plenty of space,' said Pip. 'We'll fix up some nice select little sitting-out nooks, Nell, and they will take off the superfluous population.'

'Supper in the breakfast-room – only it *is* so small and shabby. Men, Pip's room for coats and boots; girls, yours or mine, Nell,' meditated Esther.

'We'll borrow a lot of bunting from the barracks; if father won't go to the trouble of asking for it I'll ask Colonel Holcombe,' said Nell. 'Chinese lanterns on the trees all over the garden – they are *very* cheap. Oh, *won't* it all look lovely!'

'Fireworks!' cried Peter. 'Oh, mother, we can have fireworks, can't we? Catherine-wheels fixed on to all the trees, and I'll go round lighting them. We'll get them out of our pounds.'

'And me,' said Essie jealously, 'I can light half, can't I, movvie?'

'My dear little chickens, you will both have to be in bed,' said Esther.

''Tisn't *your* funeral,' said Bunty. Nellie comforted them lovingly. She would make them the loveliest little party in the world the next day with all the things left over. They should have it under the trees, and ask three children each to it.

'I pick to ask Jack next door,' cried Essie, speedily assuaged.

'She isn't to, is she, mother?' said Peter. 'He's my friend. He never asks you in to see his dog eat a rat.'

'He does, he would,' contended Essie; 'you had to give

49

him all your piece of coconut – if I hadn't eaten mine he'd have let me come too.'

'Wouldn't,' said Peter. 'He said you were only a girl. Yah!'

They went away to quarrel undisturbed, Esther entering a shuddering protest at this point.

CHAPTER SEVEN

Revelry by Night

'And silver white the river gleams,
As if Diana, in her dreams,
Had dropt her silver bow
Upon the meadows low.'

'More than my brothers are to me.'

The night of nights had come at last. Misrule was ablaze
with light. It seemed as if a fairy's magic fingers had
touched all within doors, for the shabbiness had all
fallen away somewhere, and nothing but brightness was
visible.

Such a polish on the dancing-floor! Bunty had scraped
up a whole packet of candles, and the others had bruised
themselves black and blue with sliding about to make it
'slippery'. For the three days the carpets had been up in
the double room Nellie had permitted no rest to anyone.
Did Poppet fling herself idly on a chair for a moment, did
Peter and Essie attempt to waste their breath playing
chasings she was behind them in a moment.

'Oh,' she would entreat, 'that floor will be as heavy as
possible, *do* go and fill in your time with sliding on it.'

51

And bumps and bangs would begin again instantly in the big empty room.

Oh, the armfuls of greenery Bunty cut! The fireplaces and overmantels stood out, banks of spring, trailed across with wild clematis, yellow and white roses, starry jasmine. Nellie had insisted on a yellow effect in these two rooms, and daffodils, buttercups, jonquils, nodded their sunny heads to smile approval on the charming scheme.

In the breakfast-room it was the same. You had no chance to notice that the carpet was threadbare, the sideboard of common design and scratched and battered at that, the mantelpiece mere wood, vilely ingrained to imitate marble. Your eye was arrested by this great vase where Nellie had stuck a bold branch of almond blossom, by that one where Bourbon rosebuds stood so tall, so slenderly. You stayed to admire the careless droop of that rich drapery that hung on the wall – a curtain, half-lifted to display a seascape – and never knew it was the back widths of Esther's old yellow brocade dress, and was drooped there because Essie and Peter had one sinful day striven in eager emulation as to who should draw the best blue-and-green horse on the wall. And the supper-table with its yellow ribbons, and daffodils and browny leaves and 'shivery' grass, with its burden of temptingly arranged dishes, its glowing jellies, its Alpine trifles – how were you to guess at the anxious thoughts that hovered about it?

Nellie's, in an agony lest those jellies, which had hardly been stiff enough, should melt before the opening of the door. Esther's, because she had a horrible fear she had salted some of the sandwiches twice, and left some quite without flavour. Poppet's, because Peter had made one descent on the room already and carried off two of the bought cream-cakes that were crowning with an air of dignity a plate of home-made rainbow and velvet cake. Suppose he made another raid?

Bridget and Martha, in the most stylish of muslin caps and aprons (Nellie's fingers again), were carrying in stacks of little plates and silver, and giving a last polish to the tumblers. You are not to know that the coachman and Malcolm, also enlisted in the service, were waiting just in the pantry, armed with bowls of water and clean cloths, to hurriedly wash up the scanty supply of plates and cups and send them flying back to use again.

Up in Bunty's bedroom, which seemed quietest of all, Meg was putting her baby to bed in a clothes-basket, turned extempore into a cradle. She had been helping all day and was to stay the night, as there could of course be no question of his tenderly-watched babyship turning out into the night air when festivities were over and Alan was returning home.

Meg wore a graceful black lace dress that had seen no end of service on board ship and at German concerts but told no tale of it. Her face was fresh, bright and full of girlish expectation of the evening's fun; only when you looked carefully at the mouth, the eyes, and noticed the faint line across the brow, did you guess at the storm and stress of the last two or three years.

'You will help me to listen for him, won't you Poppet,' she said as she tucked up the rosebud feet, and put the wee hand, always impatient of covering, under the blanket yet again.

'Of course I will,' said Poppet. 'I'll run up after every dance. I shall have lots of time – not many will ask me, I know. Nellie says it isn't proper of me to be up at all, but it doesn't matter, does it – just for once?'

'Not a scrap,' said Meg. 'Come here and let me tie your sash, again. How nice you look, dear. Nellie really has very clever fingers, no one would think that was Esther's old white muslin; it looks as stylish as if it had just come home from one of the big shops. And that knot of cherry colour in your hair, just the right touch.'

'But I have only got on buttoned boots,' Poppet said, in a tone of much depression.

Meg looked at the small feet clad in their walking boots, carefully blackened and polished, it is true, but unmistakably walking boots.

'Haven't you any evening ones?' she said.

'I've kept wearing them to play tennis in, 'cause my sandshoes were worn out, and they are quite done for,' sighed Poppet. 'They are burst out at the sides.'

'Why didn't you tell Esther? She would have let you have new ones,' Meg said thoughtlessly. The Misrule income, whatever it had appeared to her in old days, seemed a most comfortable and elastic one now when compared with the narrow one she had to bind herself within.

'Oh,' said Poppet, 'poor Esther, I couldn't! Such hundreds of things turned up we hadn't put on the list. And I couldn't give anything to it 'cause of being in debt to the bike man. Do you think everyone will notice them much?'

Meg reassured her. 'There will be such a crowd feet will be invisible,' she said. 'Just you enjoy yourself and don't think about them.'

'I've got three dances down on my programme already,' Poppet said, eagerly displaying her card. 'Pip has promised me one, and Bunty's going to give me two – unless the Chinese lanterns keep going out or flaring up, he has to look after them, you know. Do you think if I begged hard Alan would give me just one? Or he could halve one and just give me a turn or two.'

Meg answered for Alan – if he came at all, and no one sent for him to go back – a sadly unlikely thing.

Bunty came striding up to his looking-glass again. He had shaved this evening – almost for the first time, and was horribly self-conscious about it. Also the white tie he had borrowed from Pip fidgeted him, and he had twice split his white gloves.

'I've a good mind to turn in and not show up at all,' he said, gloomily regarding himself. 'Everyone else will have dress suits on; mine isn't even black.'

'It's such a very dark blue it looks black,' said Meg, 'and it would be useless for you to get a proper dress suit till you have finished growing. Truly, old fellow, it is as right as anything, especially as the dance is in our own house.'

'But you feel such an ass with gloves on,' said Bunty, glowering at his hands. 'You feel as if everyone's looking at you. There, look at the fools of things, they've split again – hurry up and sew them again, will you?'

'You keep stretching and twisting them so,' Meg said, getting out her needle to him for the third time. 'Try to forget them, and just be as natural with the girls as you are with us.'

'Oh, that's all very well,' said Bunty, 'but what in the world can I talk about to a girl I've only just met? You just say, "May I have this dance?" and she says, "Yes" – if she doesn't say no, thinking I look the right cut to crush her feet to jellies – and then what on earth is there left to say?'

'Oh, you say it's a warm evening, and isn't the floor nice,

55

and have you been to the theatre?' said Poppet, who had also been trying to learn up 'conversation'.

Bunty still looked unhappy. 'Yes, I know those things,' he said, 'but they don't take a jiffy to say, and then all the rest of the time you *can't* think of a word to say, however you cudgel your head.'

'But the girl generally gives you an opening, doesn't she?' said Meg. 'And once you've got fairly started isn't it all right?'

'Oh,' said Bunty, 'she generally says, "How sweet your sister Nellie looks!" or "What a lot here tonight!" but that doesn't keep you going for long. I often wish I had Pip's knack, he's a smart fellow, that chap, Meg; I often watch him, and his lips never seem to stop moving all the time. And he can make a girl laugh no end. I'll always be an ass at talking.'

'Oh no,' said Meg, handing back the glove, 'it comes with practice. At your age Pip had just as little to say. But do your best to forget all about yourself, and try to give the girl as nice a time as you can.'

The first ring sounded through the house, and a flutter and thrill went with it. Bunty, who was just going out on the landing, dived back into his room again, and flattened himself against the wall lest anyone ascending the stairs should catch a glimpse of him. Poppet rushed importantly off to the bedroom to be ready with her delightful distribution of the pretty programmes.

Essie and Peter crept out of bed where they were lying very wide-awake, and stole in their nightgowns to a corner of the landing where they squeezed together and giggled and squeaked and admired the opera-cloaks, and fondly imagined they could not be seen.

Nellie, anxiously contemplating the jellies once more,

beat a hasty retreat to be in readiness in the drawing-room to help Esther and her father receive. Nellie in cloudy white, with white jasmine in her shining hair, with fair young arms and tenderly moulded white neck and shoulders, with dewy, lovely eyes, and a most exquisite, excited pink in her cheeks!

A man – Nellie's 'real man', going upstairs to the cloak-room, caught a glimpse of this vision and smiled to himself approvingly.

'Shows up even better by night than day,' he told himself. 'I'm not so sorry I came after all.'

While he changed his boots and removed his overcoat he looked a little superciliously around at the eager fellows who were doing the same. Friends of Pip's most of them were, embryo doctors and lawyers, University students, all very young and anxious to enjoy themselves, many head over heels in love with the white vision downstairs, and burning to inscribe her name on their programmes. They lost no time in getting on their patent leather shoes, and dragging on their gloves, and 'settling' their ties; quite an army seemed to present themselves to Nellie at one and the same moment, so determined was each not to be last.

But the blue eyes glanced at the door once or twice, over their heads, in the pauses of introductions, and saw that all the girls had their programmes well on the way to being filled.

And when he came in coolly, languidly, what a throb her heart gave, what a tumult of sweet colour rushed into her face! Nearly all the girls were looking at him, and with eyes so clearly admiring, their partners could have gnashed their teeth.

Almost a head taller than anyone in the room he stood,

finely made, distinguished looking. A black moustache with a military cut about it hid his lips, but not the cynical lines around them that thrilled these girls; dark eyes, with a somewhat bored, melancholy expression in them, looked out at you.

This was Captain Reginald Morton, who had been invalided home from the Transvaal with a sufficient amount of commendation for courage to make society delighted to pet him as a hero. He was enjoying the petting.

Nellie gave him a dance. Those eager youths had left her only one, and when he begged so hard for a second, what could she do but cross off Bunty's name and give him that space?

'But they are both together,' she objected, 'six and seven.'

'That is as it should be,' he returned. 'I shall enjoy six so much, it would be impossible for me to give you up for seven. We shall sit the second one out and talk to each other.'

Nellie moved through her crowded rooms with a fluttering heart.

Bunty caught at her for one second. 'It's my left arm I offer the girls, not the right, isn't it?' he whispered anxiously.

'Yes,' said Nellie, starting guiltily.

The evening danced along. The floor repaid every bump and bruise it had caused; the jellies melted not; Esther's sandwich fears were groundless; and the trifle promised to stand out against the most repeated attacks, to Bunty's great relief.

In the earlier part of the evening a moon swam out, and helped the soft pink and green lanterns to make the old garden and the sleeping river incredibly beautiful. But later she drew a discreet veil over her kindly face, and the grounds were full of sweet shadows, and happy young love was able to whisper its tale in this nook Pip had made among the tree-ferns – on that shaky seat beneath the Japanese maple, there on the grass bank where heavy magnolias intoxicated the air.

Perhaps the programme had an unrehearsed event or two. As when Peter, compelled to just two more cream-cakes, miscalculated his time and the music stopped and the breathless, laughing guests trooped out to halls and staircases and verandahs, just as his small figure in its grey and pink pyjamas came stealing from the supper-room, booty in hand.

And when Essie's shrill pipe floated down from a landing –

'Oh, just look at father dancing – oh, doesn't he look funny!'

And when Meg came into the room with a scared face and sought out Nellie, and then Poppet, and then Bunty, and then Pip, to ask whisperingly what they had done with Baby, and please, please not to play jokes, as he would catch a dreadful cold being out of bed so long.

And when at their genuinely innocent faces she faced round and rushed out of the room so wildly, the guests thought there was a fire at least somewhere, but were able to smile relievedly when Pip came back from the short frantic search and reported a baby had been lost but was now found.

As indeed it was, in Essie's little bed, between herself and Peter, who had deserted his own couch – snuggled down so closely that Meg's first flying visit had never revealed the fact, and the trio continued its peaceful slumbers while the agonised mother and blank-faced sisters and brothers rushed hither and thither, looking under beds, behind doors and similar unlikely places, and downstairs the guests wondered and waited.

One o'clock and the end of the sweet evening was come. The last strains of the last dance filled the air, plaintive in its gaiety even in the dancing-room, curiously burdened with sadness as it stole out from the bright windows and wandered over the damp grass, and through the dark, midnight trees down to the place where the *Cestrum nocturnum* bushes flung out the sweetness they keep alone for night.

'I must go back to the house,' Nellie said. 'Everyone will be going in a minute.'

She stood up from the rickety seat Bunty had contrived so merrily that very morning.

'No, no,' her partner said, 'you shall not go – a little longer – a little longer.' He caught her hand in its white suede glove and held it prisoner. 'See how helpless you are,' he murmured, 'you cannot move unless I let you.'

Nellie tried to release her trembling hand.

'How foolish you are, Captain Morton,' she said, with a laugh, quite her ordinary laugh she persuaded herself. 'I must go – the girls will be waiting for me to say goodbye.'

But still he held her. 'I too am waiting,' he said softly, and looked down at her with tender eyes. To kiss the exquisite curve of the girl's young cheek seemed to him at the moment the most desirable thing in life.

And yet he hesitated – hesitated as he seldom had done before when he had wanted such a thing as a conclusion to a dance.

'Nellie!' he said.

A shy, frightened dignity came to Nell, she withdrew her hand, stepped away from the seat.

'Listen,' she said, 'someone is playing "God save the King". I must go at once.'

He walked along the path with her, the path where the last of the lantern candles was spluttering to a lingering death. He had not what he desired, yet he assured himself he was more in love with the child than ever.

At the door he paused one minute. 'I shall never forget this evening – never,' he said, close to her ear, in his deep rather melancholy voice that had said the same thing so often, so often.

Nellie slipped up to the lighted bedrooms, and laughed with her girlfriends, and helped them on with their cloaks, and said goodbye to them with almost hysterical nervousness.

Such eyes, such flushed cheeks, such a strange little trembling mouth! But how could any of them know just what had happened to her?

CHAPTER EIGHT

The Other Side of the Fence

Adjoining the Misrule grounds stood a gloomy, ugly house where never a tenant stayed longer than a year at a time, and the average one found three or six months sufficient occupancy.

The same river as at Misrule danced before it - the same air sweetened it, the same birds sang.

But the architect had evidently conceived it in a saddened moment; the chief living-rooms looked out on the sunless, viewless side, the verandah roofs sloped down as if their only object in life was to cut off light and sun from all windows; the grey, porous stones of the walls, even in the summer, seemed saturated with the river's damps and mists. There were too many trees in the grounds, stiff, depressing pines for the most part - that, planted to make a girdle of privacy, grown now to maturity made prison bars instead.

This tenant left because his children had sore throats or bad chests from the moment of entering the place; that one flung up his lease, after striving to re-let, because rheumatism attacked him the hour the winter westerlies set in; this one went off in a hurry because his wife became morbid and nervous in the place.

The rueful landlord was just considering a scheme that included a wholesale chopping down of the pines and a general letting in of the sunshine, when a lady came along, examined it very thoughtfully, and offered not only to occupy it, but – a thing the landlord's rosiest dreams never expected to realise – to buy it.

Peter and Essie and Poppet were pleasurably excited, as they were with each fresh tenant, when movements of life began about the old house.

Despite Esther's remonstrances they peeped through and over the fence, and from the staircase window which alone gave a glimpse of the house, until they had gleaned all the information they wanted.

Yes, there were some children. A girl and a boy, Peter and Essie said; two girls and one boy, Poppet maintained.

'Pooh, you only saw her twice,' said Peter. 'What was your other girl like?'

'About as old as me,' said Poppet, 'and she had the loveliest golden hair and a big white hat.'

'Why,' said Peter, 'that was the same one – wasn't it, Essie?'

Essie upheld him. Of course it was the same girl; she had buttoned boots on and grey gloves.

'They both had,' persisted Poppet. 'When the carriage door opened and the boy and one girl got out, I saw quite plainly through my crack another girl, just like the other one, jump out and run up the steps.'

But they only jeered at her and said she saw double. Indeed Poppet's 'other girl' was a standing joke in the house afterwards for some time, for when speech and language became established between the two houses and Peter demanded 'wasn't there someone else to play with?' both boy and girl said no at once.

Poppet also reported that first day that there was a lady with flashing eyes and a gentleman with a red face. Peter endorsed this statement; at least he agreed to there being a man and a woman, but he hadn't noticed the red face or the flashing eyes.

Then an excited statement that they all three tried to make at once. No women servants to do by that old stone house as Martha and Bridget did by Misrule, but instead one, two, three inky black New Guinea boys – two of men's stature, one of Bunty's age perhaps. And in the months that followed and during which the intimacy between the two houses progressed chiefly through or over the dividing fence no other woman was ever seen about the place.

After giving the newcomers time to settle comfortably down Esther called for neighbourliness, though she knew nothing of them but that they were from Queensland, where they had owned a large station, and that their name was Saville.

Nellie went with her – laden with commission from Poppet to be sure to find out the name of the sweet little girl with golden hair, and how far she was in music, and did she play with dolls still.

'And you might ask the boy to come in and have a game,'

said Peter. 'It's pretty sick for me only having Essie to play with always.'

Esther and Nellie went up the long drive to the house, and stepped into the girdle of pine trees past which the sun came not. They rang the bell.

'Missa Saville not at home,' said the black boy who opened the door – indeed he began to say his speech, as if a lesson learned by rote, before they even asked him.

Esther handed out cards. He looked at them doubtfully, then took them into one great black hand, and with the other closed the door before they had turned their faces round.

Feeling a trifle snubbed they descended the steps and crossed the path again; and so noiselessly fell their footsteps on the thick carpet of pine needles that the lady of the house, walking bareheaded among the trees with her boy and girl, did not hear them approach.

It was an awkward moment. Esther and Nellie would have been grateful for just one more second to put a space between them that would have excused exchange of courtesies, but they were actually face to face.

The lady looked at them haughtily; Nellie was ever after able to attest Poppet's statement about flashing eyes.

Esther mentioned her name, and said something pleasant about being next-door neighbours and so on. She even had her hand extended.

But Mrs Saville barely touched it. 'I must ask you to excuse me,' she said. 'I never see visitors.'

'Oh, mamma,' said a choked little voice beside her, 'they live next door – the dear little girl with brown hair – oh, mamma!'

Esther and Nellie caught a glimpse of a little beseeching

face with sensitive lips and eyes full of quick tears at their rebuff. They could have picked her up and kissed her, so small she looked, so distressed, so lovely with her filmy gold hair making tender sunlight against those dark pines.

Esther's colour was perhaps a shade warmer than usual.

'You must excuse us,' she said, 'it was unfortunate, but of course we had no means of knowing. Good afternoon.'

'Good afternoon,' said Mrs Saville. They turned and went down the drive again at once.

'Oh, mamma,' they heard the quivering little voice say again.

Past the curve that hid the house they began to recover themselves a little.

'I never felt so small in all my life,' said Nell. 'I feel crushed, trodden to earth. What a horribly insulting, ill-bred woman!'

'I'm not sure if those are quite the right adjectives,' said Esther, 'but it was not a pleasant experience certainly. I feel distinctly snubbed myself, still – '

'I believe you would make excuses for the fiend himself, Esther,' Nellie said hotly, 'it was horribly ill-bred. And that sweet little girl – she isn't fit to be her mother.'

'A dear little child,' said Esther, 'but how fragile she looked. I should like to have whipped her up and carried her off for a romp.'

Was ever such a chapter of accidents? They had been overheard – a man was sitting, his back to a gum-tree, his coat so nearly the colour of the bark, he had been completely merged to them in the general colour-scheme around. It was the one-time squatter himself, come to smoke his pipe where pines were not and the sun shone as it listed.

He stood up and looked at them awkwardly – his face showed them he had heard. As Esther said afterwards all words deserted her; she never felt so inclined in all her life to pick up her dress and run straight out of an unpleasant situation.

She tried to pretend she did not see the man coming towards her; she began to hurry, talking very fast to Nell.

But he came right into their pathway, and held out his hand with such an unhappy, anxious look on his kindly face, they were both touched.

'You are our neighbours, aren't you?' he said – 'Mrs and Miss Woolcot? Most kind of you to look us up – most kind. I thank you sincerely.'

Esther shook hands mechanically. She had an idea afterwards that she murmured something about it being a fine afternoon, but Nellie opined she had said unsteadily it looked like rain.

The poor fellow agreed to whatever she said. 'I'm afraid you did not find Mrs Saville at home,' he added.

'No,' said Esther, her colour warming again.

'I am sorry,' he said, 'most sorry. She – she never is at home.' He sighed heavily.

Esther's self-consciousness began to fade. She said a warm word or two of his beautiful little girl; she laughed and told him she had a little step-daughter at home who she believed dreamed nightly about her.

'Ah!' he said delightedly, 'is that the little brown-haired thing? Lylie and I call her the Elf; we watch her playing from a window or the fence. I – forgive the question, Mrs Woolcot, but would you mind telling me her name? My little girl spends half her time wondering what it is.'

'Poppet,' said Esther. 'She was christened Winifred, but we always call her Poppet.'

'Poppet,' said the old fellow, 'I won't forget. And – and – you will smile at me for asking, but the answer would delight my poor little girl so much – do you mind telling me what sums she does, and whether she has given up playing yet with dolls?'

There was something pathetic here – some sad shadow born of those dreadful pine trees. Esther's throat swelled a little as she looked at the quiet-faced man asking this simple question. She forgot her snub – everything but the fact that there was unhappiness somewhere.

'Couldn't she come in and play with my little girl?' she said. 'Poppet talks of her all day. We would take great care of her.'

The man's face grew extremely unhappy again. 'Very sorry,' he said, 'most sorry – her – her mother – thinks better not – never allows her – very sorry.'

Esther was very gentle. 'Forgive me,' she said. 'I did not know. Tell little Lylie that Poppet does compound multiplication – badly, and is just beginning reduction, and that she has at least eleven dolls that she loves passionately. Now we will say good afternoon.'

'Good afternoon,' said Mr Saville sadly.

After this episode, however, he constantly stopped Poppet when he met her walking up the River Road or riding on her ramshackle bicycle, and quite a friendship grew up between them, though Lylie was still as unattainable as ever.

At first his questions seemed curious to Poppet, but after a time she grew quite accustomed to answering them, and used even to interrogate him herself.

As, for instance, when he inquired whether her dolls had party dresses as well as day dresses, and if she put frills on their bonnets or only plain lace, and did she make their shoes herself? She would reply yes, certainly, all of them, yes to the frills, yes to the shoes. And had Lylie a boy doll at all, and had she any with brown eyes or were they all blue, and had she begun to make their winter frocks yet?

One day Saville had a delightful proposition to make. It was that a doll of Lylie's should come on a visit to Poppet's, and one of Poppet's go in exchange to Lylie.

Poppet was charmed with the idea. Then she paused suddenly. 'But will the flashing-eyed lady allow her?' she blurted out, and then grew red, and made a stumbling apology and said 'Mrs Saville'.

'Oh, that will be all right – you needn't think of that,' the father said reassuringly. Though, if the truth were known, he was more than a little nervous as to his success in smuggling one waxen lady out of the house and introducing another into Lylie's family without his wife's knowledge. Still it was his little girl's own idea, and she was so very eager about it.

Poppet asked for two days' preparation.

'Cherry's clothes will have to be washed,' she said frankly, 'and some of them mended. But I will have her ready by Thursday.'

All Misrule was interested in the exchange and had a look at the departing Cherry. She was a rather attenuated doll, with a painful red smile, blue eyes (one cracked across), and hair so thin she habitually wore a close cap. But she was bravely dressed today, and bore in a bundle beside her a complete change of underclothes, a party frock, a second bonnet, and another pair of shoes.

The doll from the Pines came to hand, no one knowing it had been forced to travel as far as the gate inside a large silk umbrella. It came accompanied by a miniature tin trunk, a wee Paris hat-box, and a little dressing-case containing comb, brush, hairpins and even powder-puff. And such beautiful clothes, fine Liberty silk exquisitely tucked and embroidered! The doll itself was not painfully new, you could see it had been kissed and carried and played with these many days.

But Poppet stared at the work in the clothes.

'Can Lylie really sew as well as that?' she said, quite awed.

'Oh no,' said Saville, 'her mother makes those for her. She is a wonderful needlewoman, there is nothing she can't do.' He spoke proudly.

It took Misrule a little time to readjust its ideas and picture the insulting, 'flashing-eyed' lady, sitting stitch, stitching at these patient little clothes.

CHAPTER NINE

Which Revolves Around a Rat

Lylie was too spiritual and at the same time too spiritless to attempt to protest against her mother's wishes, but Jack the seven-year-old brother was just a healthy and perfectly ordinary little boy. From the hour he discovered the next-door Peter – Peter engaged in exercising the fowls with a three-legged race – no power had been able to keep him quite away from the dividing fence. He was either pressed up close against it with his eye to a knot-hole, or sitting astride it, or poking bits of whittled wood or marbles or tops to Peter through a place where the wood had shrunk up an inch or two away from the ground.

It was he who extended the invitation to watch the closing scene in the life of a rat.

And Peter had accepted it in the noble spirit in which it had been offered. He swarmed over without a word of ado – it never occurred to *him* to inquire whether his visit might be distasteful to the lady of the house.

'Come on,' he said, 'where is it? In your kitchen? If it is some silly idiot will go and open the door and you'll have lost it.'

Jack said 'H'sh', and gave a troubled glance at his house. 'Lie down flat,' he said. 'Yes, like that. Can you crawl that way up to the stables? If she sees you, you'll have to go.'

Peter progressed along cheerfully on his hands and knees, close to the fence, for a hundred feet or so.

'Now you can stand up,' Jack said, and Peter became relievedly upright once more, for they were well behind the sheltering walls of the stables.

They spent an exhilarating hour in the corn-room setting the rat at liberty, and then urging on the eager fox terrier to the chase.

Jack, from long training, only hurrahed softly at exciting periods, but Peter, accustomed to freest shoutings and yellings in Misrule paddocks – who could expect *him* to modulate his voice?

The unusual noise penetrated into the grey kitchen, and presently down came the youngest of the New Guinea boys to suppress it.

'You clear out of this, Charlie,' said Jack boldly, showing off before his new friend.

'Young white boy better go home straight way off,' Charlie said. But he was only sixteen, and when the rat rushed up the wall and leapt a corn box, and used an old saddle for a bridge to take him to the comparative safety of a low rafter, Charlie leaned with his elbows on a bin and became as absorbed as the other boys.

Down came the inky cook and banged Charlie about

the head as a preliminary rite. Charlie grinned cheerfully, and Peter waxed bold at the sight. There was nothing alarming after all about these black-faced fellows – indeed an ebony smile seemed a good deal merrier and more boyish a thing than a white one. Peter stood his ground.

'I'll go home when he's caught,' he said, and gave another yell and rushed after the terrier and kicked his excited heels on any and every sounding zinc box in the place. Down came the gardener. Peter mocked at him from the vantage ground of a beam up to which he had swung himself. His humour for all alien races was the same.

'Welly ni cabbagee – allee flesh cabbagee,' he said.

The sable-handed gardener adjured him, in very respectable English, to return to his own dwelling.

'Tleepence – no feah – too muchee money,' replied Peter.

The cook stepped on to a box and tried to dislodge the invader by force.

'You, boy Charlie, climb up other side,' he said, and the boy Charlie, grinning, went to obey.

But Peter, agile as any monkey, swarmed up higher still.

'Muchee fine cabbagee,' he said, 'sick-a-pen, all li, some oder day, eh?'

'I say,' said Jack, 'you'd better go – here's mother coming.'

Peter dropped down among the black boys like a plummet.

'Isn't there another door?' he said, with a hunted look round.

Jack gave his head a melancholy shake.

'Get out of the way, then,' said Peter, and made a dash at the door and reached it and sprang across the path, and shot over the grass and scraped up over his own fence all in less than one minute.

He even had his foot planted ready for further flight, lest his own territory should not be sufficient and the strong-hold of his walls be required for absolute safety. But the lady showed no signs of climbing after him. With his eye to the hole in the fence he saw her returning to the house, Jack walking dejectedly before her, and the dark-faced procession behind.

Three days, however, sufficed for the recovery of Jack's spirit, and he was at the fence again, making that cheerful hole a little larger with a bit of sharp iron. By the time Peter had – for his mind's health that morning – stated the fact, in bad writing and worse Latin, that 'the Gauls laid waste the lands of the Romans far and wide' and 'before all others Demosthenes and Cicero were the most renowned orators'; had wrestled with the wretched rhyme of masculine exceptions to the rule that the termination *is* is feminine –

> 'Panis, piscis, crinis, finis,
> Ignis, lapis, pulvis, cinis,
> Orbis, amvis and canalis,
> Sanguis, unguis, glis, annalis';

had limped miserably through the French verb *to boil*, and been rendered vacant-eyed by the statement that it was a *neuter* verb, and with its literal meaning only used in the infinitive, preceded by the verb *faire* in any tense and person whenever the subject was a noun (or a pronoun) referring to a person; had sat through, along with Poppet, while Essie merely wrote a baby copy, an object lesson on the composition of the air, and had his brain stunned with phrases like 'carbon dioxide, nitrogen, oxygen, component elements, molecules' – by the time he had undergone and overcome all these wearinesses and gone dashing out, Essie at his heels, to the fence, lo the knot-hole was large enough for you to shake hands through and see each other's faces in quarterly sections, instead of sixteenthly as heretofore.

'Did you get it on Monday?' he inquired.

'No, it got loose again,' said Jack.

Peter had forgotten the rat. He was inquiring after the punishment that he expected had been meted out to his suffering friend, for Poppet's imagination had seen him stretched on a species of inquisitorial rack in a dark cellar, and Essie had opined that he had been thrashed with a cat-o'-nine tails like the stowaway in Peter's book.

'Oh,' said Jack laconically, when the delicate inquiry was repeated, 'had to learn a page of exports and imports – no, that was for telling a stuffer about the tarts – had to sit on a stool for an hour – no, that was for shouting up the staircase – oh, forget what it was – come on, what'll we do?'

Peter cast about for an employment, but it was the woman who tempted him to the fall.

'*You* come over *here*,' said Essie.

Jack and Peter both looked a trifle diffident.

'Where is she?' asked Peter nervously.

'Gone out in the Box,' said Jack. (It was by this slighting term he referred to the expensive closed brougham in which his mother took a daily drive.)

'Oh, well, come on,' said Peter relievedly. He had had an unpleasant vision at the moment of Essie's suggestion, of the tall figure striding across their own safe, sunny paddocks in vengeful pursuit of her son. But safe in the Box!

'Come on,' he said, 'you'd better not lose any time, or she may come back.'

Jack, urged thus by two, put a half-fearful foot into the

75

hole, and then the rest was so easy he was over in a new world in a second, his conscience cast behind him as a snake sheds its skin.

'And I can shout as much as I like, you said I could,' was his first remark.

'Of course you can,' Peter said, staring at him.

But it took Essie, accustomed as she was to Peter's racket, a little time to get used to the yells and halloos and hurrahs with which the small youth from the other side of the fence sought to let off his long-suppressed steam.

Indeed, so very unusual were the noises, that Esther actually put on her garden-hat at last and went down the long paddock to the shed to make quite sure her two children were not hanging by their tortured hair to the rafters, or being burnt at the stake.

'Why, who is this?' she exclaimed, 'and what *are* you doing to him, Peter? Have you been fighting the poor little fellow?'

All three laughed cheerfully for answer.

'But,' said Esther, troubled, 'my dear little boy, I can't let you stay here, though I should like to. You know your mother will not allow you to come and play.'

Peter and Essie sighed impatiently – why could not Esther have stayed up in the quiet house where there were no problems for her moral senses to wrestle with?

Jack looked at her quietly. He was a pale, rather stunted-looking little lad, with Lylie's expression, but very wise eyes. He opened his lips.

'Mother's compliments and would you mind letting me stay in your place for a little while this morning, so I can shout as much as I like?'

Peter and Essie stared at their new friend with blank

76

faces; their own moral rectitude had been so carefully attended to by Esther that they found it hard to grasp such an astonishing want of principle.

But Esther was a very unsuspicious woman and looked merely relieved.

'I shall be very pleased to have you,' she said. 'Stay as long as you like and shout as much as you like.'

'Why won't you be let shout at your house?' asked Peter. 'Does it make her head ache?'

'It's not her,' said Jack, fondling the latest guinea pig, 'it's the secret.'

'What secret?' demanded the two children eagerly.

But Jack looked cautious again instantly. 'Don't let's waste time,' he said. 'Let's do something,' and Esther, thus dismissed, returned to the house.

'Why didn't you tell us she said you could come?' demanded Peter.

But Jack merely gave a peculiar wink he had copied from Charlie, and went on stirring up the little sleepy guinea pigs.

The luncheon bell rang. Peter and Essie dragged their guest up to the house.

'He says he can stay to dinner,' they said.

Esther duly expressed her sense of honour and delight, and drew up a chair for him at the table, and asked Martha to bring another knife and fork and a tumbler.

'But you must promise to let me go at two,' he said. 'That's the time we have dinner, and I wouldn't like the pater to be lonely. What room's your pater having his dinner in?'

Esther was busily engaged carving the roast mutton, and Nellie with three vegetables to apportion also had her attention distracted.

It was Poppet who answered that her father was away in town, at the barracks, and only came home for late dinner.

'Do you take it in turns to stop with him?' asked the guest.

Peter replied that his father and mother and Pip and Nellie and Bunty all had dinner together. Jack digested the information thoughtfully.

'It must look funny,' he said.

'What must?' said Esther, resting on her oars a little moment.

'You and him having dinner in the same room,' returned Jack.

Esther looked puzzled, but returned to her labours.

'Don't your father and mother?' said Poppet curiously.

''Course they don't,' said Jack. 'Mother has hers in the study, and father has his in the breakfast-room. And Lylie and me takes it in turns where we have it. I had breakfast with mother, so I'll have lunch with pater.'

Esther looked troubled, for everyone was listening now. 'Jack, dear,' she said gently, 'when you come here you mustn't tell us things that go on at your house – no gentleman does that – just talk about your games and pets and things like that.'

'What did I say?' demanded Jack aggrievedly. 'I've not told you anything. I never let out a word about the secret.'

'What pets have you at home?' asked Esther, striving to steer into safe waters.

'There's my dog Blinker,' said Jack, 'and on the station I used to have a kangaroo what would eat out of my hand, only then it got cranky and father sent it away. Wish I had a little kangaroo now.'

'Why don't you get your mamma to ask your father to

78

let you have another?' asked Essie, who was always making use of an ambassador herself.

Jack looked at her scornfully. 'What a silly you are!' he said. 'How could she when they don't speak to each other, scarcely never? Only when Lylie gets ill, or that time I fell out a window, and when – '

'Baked apples, Jack?' cried Esther, 'and rice to them, and cream? Pass this to Jack, Poppet. The apples are from the orchard and the cream from that nice brown-and-white cow you were admiring.'

'I'll have the cream,' said Jack, 'and if you've got a little cake I can scoop it out and fill it up and it'll be a cream-cake. You can give the apples and rice to him,' and he pointed a careless finger at Peter.

'But I should like you to have something substantial,' said Esther.

'Oh, I'm keeping myself a bit hungry,' said Jack. 'Tairoa was making jellied things with meat inside them, and I always help father eat them, 'cause mother thinks he likes them a lot and gen'ally looks to see if he's emptied the dish. One time when she had been crying a lot – '

'Jack,' said Esther, 'it is two o'clock, you had better run off at once.'

Jack rose at once and gave a glance through the open window.

'You didn't happen to see that Box thing of ours go past yet, did you?' he asked.

'He means their buggy with the big lid,' said Essie.

'No,' said Esther, 'but I think you had better go now, dear.'

'All right, but I'll come another day,' promised the guest, and went off munching the remains of his improvised cream-cake.

CHAPTER TEN

Res Angustæ

'Then give me leave that I may turn the key,
That no man enter till my tale be done.'

'I'm afraid that I've hardly got this wide enough,' Alan said, and stood back with a somewhat anxious air to survey his afternoon's handiwork. 'Suppose you want to get a really big joint in some time, Meg?'

Meg laughed. 'Suppose something a little more likely,' she said. 'Our butcher would really have a severe shock if he got an order for a joint from us that had not the strict proviso attached, "Not more than five pounds".'

'But you have to allow for the dish too,' Alan said.

'Our pantry holds no dish that would refuse to go through that door,' said Meg.

'Oh, well,' said Alan, and took up his hammer again, relief on his face, 'that's all right. I've almost finished.'

'You are quite sure the door will fit so that no flies or ants can get through?' Meg said, and examined the hinges with much care. 'I lose so much meat this dreadful weather.'

Alan glanced unhappily at the cheerful crevice or two that plainly showed. 'Couldn't you paste a bit of mosquito net over?' he said. 'I'm afraid I can't make it fit better.'

'Perhaps I can manage,' said Meg. 'Hush, wasn't that the bell? Oh, Alan, I'm sure it is a patient this time – it isn't a bit like a hawker's ring. Oh, Alan, if only it is!'

Alan had laid down his saw and his hammer and was gazing with painful expectancy at the back door. Meg's colour went and came in waves. Oh, the quick, bright hopes that leapt up in her each time that loud gong sounded through the house, and oh how often they were quenched!

Lizzie, in her neat equipment of goffered cap and apron, crossed the yard.

'Two nuns collecting for the Hospice of St Margaret, ma'am,' she said.

'Hang the Hospice of St Margaret!' was Alan's pious ejaculation, and he picked up his saw again and began to look for his pencil mark on the length of wood in front of him.

Meg's colour was quiet again. 'Tell them I am sorry, but I have too many calls on my purse,' she said, 'and I hope you are listening to Baby, Lizzie.'

'He's sleeping like a lamb yet,' said Lizzie. 'I'm sitting on the verandah near him while I cut my papers for the shelves.' She went back through the house to the front door to bear the disheartening news of refusal to the sable-clad sisters waiting there.

Alan's hammer smote the quiet air of the yard from time to time, and the movable meat-safe that the summer demanded and the household purse refused to afford approached nearer and nearer to completion.

It was not a very neat job – indeed Bunty, who was clever

with the tools of carpentry, made the mental comment of 'clumsy, hulking thing' when he saw it. But Meg had been so worried with the difficulty of keeping the meat good and Baby's milk sweet in this little inconvenient house, that the young doctor had laid down the scalpel which never had use enough, and picked up an unfamiliar saw.

'It's time I knew better how to use these tools,' he said as he worked. 'There must be many things you want, Girlie, though you never worry me to make them.'

'Oh,' said Meg, 'till Bunty got this bicycle fever there was no need, he did all I wanted. But I am certainly just beginning to find out what a violet he was to me.'

'What else do you want?' Alan said. 'I've spare time enough, Heaven knows, to build furniture for half-a-dozen houses. What shall I start with? You shall not be worried for want of the ordinary decencies of life.'

'But I'm afraid it would hardly do for Lizzie to see you wasting time over such things,' said Meg gravely. 'She would tell the baker, and the frightful scandal would spread through the suburb. As long as you are out or in the consulting room among your books, she considers you are respectably employed. But making meat-safes! I'm sure if she sickened with measles tonight she would make me send for some other doctor.'

'Hang Lizzie!' said Alan, 'you shall not go without things you want for her. You can give her to understand hammering is my hobby. Now, deliver your orders.'

Meg had been made comfortable on a cushion placed at one end of the rough carpenter's bench Alan had improvised for himself in the wood and coal shed. She looked up from the baby bonnet she was trying to construct from a white silk blouse of her own.

'I should *love* to have a toy cupboard for Little Boy,' she said, with pleased eyes. 'Pip and the others give him so many things the house seems strewn with his toys.'

'That's one – what else?'

'Oh, if you *could* make another wide set of shelves for me to put clothes on,' Meg said, 'your good coat ought not to hang, it gets so shapeless. And where to put my starched blouses and Boy's pelisses after I have ironed them I don't know.'

'After *you* have ironed them!' Alan repeated sharply. 'Surely Lizzie can iron!'

Meg was swift to cover her slip. 'Of course she can,' she said, 'all the uninteresting things. Baby's things and my pretty blouses are specialities I like to attend to myself. There's the bell again – this really *might* be someone, mightn't it? A nice wealthy old man with rheumatism, or a messenger to say scarlet fever has broken out at the boarding school on the hill. Oh no, not scarlet fever, because you might bring it home to Baby. Something harmless but lengthy – an epidemic of sprained ankles, for instance.' She talked lightly, quickly, but with anxious eyes all the time on the back door through which Lizzie seemed so long in appearing.

'Oh, it is the children,' she said, pleasure and disappointment both in her voice as Poppet first and then Bunty appeared in the doorway.

Such a pair of hot, red faces! It was a heatwave day. The thermometer had gone steadily from 85°F to 96°F in the shade during the afternoon, but a trifle like that never kept those particular wheels idle in the Misrule hall.

'Where's your seltzogene?' said Bunty. 'I'll empty it for you in five minutes.' He looked around thirstily as if expecting to find it in the wood shed. Poppet reminded him with a delicate poke of her elbow of the fact that seltzogenes are luxuries, costing money for both purchase and keeping up, and therefore strangers in this little household.

'Or water'll do just as well,' said Bunty, recollecting. 'A tap and a tumbler are all I crave. Hope you don't have a water meter here Meg – if you have you'll find I've made a big difference in your bill in a minute or two.'

'I've lemons,' cried Meg, jumping down from the bench. 'You shall have a lemon squash each in a moment. But how *could* you ride on such a day? Alan, I'm afraid you'll say there really is insanity in the family.'

'Well,' said Alan, 'and who better qualified than I to minister to such a family? Did I not make a special study in Heidelberg of brain disease, and didn't old Hamburgher once actually grunt "not bad" to my theories?'

'Who was old Hamburgher?' said Bunty.

'Only the greatest brain specialist in all the Fatherland,' said Meg, open pride on her face, 'and he thought so much of Alan's ideas he used to talk to him and argue with him for hours together.'

'Fudge,' said Alan, 'he took pity on a half-blind beggar and helped him to pass the time, that was all. Still it qualified me for dealing with Misrule madness. And these two plainly have a virulent attack. Well, my chief desire has been a really good lunacy case, and now I am happy.'

'Pooh!' said Bunty. 'The heat's nothing to make a fuss about – is it, Poppet? There's Nellie lying on the matting in the nursery and feeling it a lot more just because she keeps thinking about it. You forget all about it when you're riding, don't you, Poppet?'

'Nearly,' said Poppet, wiping her streaming, scarlet little face. 'Where's Baby, Meg?'

'On the verandah,' said Meg, standing at the kitchen table cutting her lemons; 'it is the coolest place. You like plenty of sugar, don't you, Bunty? – You take this – here is yours Poppet – I'll just run with this to Alan – sawing is hot work too.'

The cyclists drank with slow and deep enjoyment while Meg went first to Alan with his drink, then to Lizzie, who had just begun to lay the cloth for tea, which on Saturdays and Sundays always took the place of the half-past six dinner.

The cloth was very white and uncreased, pink carnations and feathery grass with wandering pink ribbon made a pleasant resting-place in the centre for the eye, and the simple white china was prettily arranged. Lizzie would presently add a plate of thinly-cut bread and butter or a stand of toast, a crisp lettuce or a small glass of some preserve. Nothing more – it was the customary tea, and with the addition of porridge the customary breakfast in the little household. But two hungry cyclists! The perturbed house-mistress went into her pantry and looked anxiously at her shelves. There was a tin of salmon there certainly, and with parsley or egg sauce it could quickly be made into an appetising dish. But it cost ninepence halfpenny! A very large sum when one remembered a tin of Bartlett pears had been opened to make out the dinner of the night before, when Andrew had come in unexpectedly; and a shilling tin of whitebait on Tuesday, when the Major had come to share, as he expressed it, 'pot luck'. Which, happening to be precisely two small cutlets, albeit they wore frills and reposed on a bed of feathered potatoes, refused to be shared. Eggs! There were just three lying in the basket – Meg had not dared to order more that morning, for they were two-and-threepence a dozen. If they were scrambled nicely and put on big slices of toast, they might appease the hungry young appetites just come. And that last jar of pineapple jam up there – Alan's eyes would brighten at the sight of it – he was *such* a school-boy for these dainties, though he professed so strongly he cared nothing for them, and had never been in better health than under the present *régime* of strictly wholesome diet. Yes, half the jar of jam and the other half would make a pudding next week – Meg took it down from its resting place.

And into the pantry came Poppet with downcast eyes and a basket.

'I just slipped these things in, Megsie, to keep my tools from rattling about,' she said. 'I haven't got a proper tool-bag, you know, so I use this basket, and it's *such* a nuisance when the oil-can and things bang about all the way.'

To prevent this nuisance she had padded the basket with a bunch of parsnips, some beetroot and French beans from the vegetable garden, several lemons from the orchard, a bottle of milk, five eggs that her own fowls had laid, and a bunch of marguerites to keep the table going until next visit. Certainly two of the eggs were broken with the jolting.

Such a weight the basket had been on the already heavy machine. Bunty often called her an obstinate little donkey for insisting on carrying such a large clumsy basket on these rides; he never dreamed it held anything heavier than the legitimate tools.

There was a tear in Meg's eye as she took out the loving little gifts and laid them on the pantry shelves. No one but Poppet realised quite how bare those shelves were, and even she always pretended the little things she brought had no particular purpose.

More than once she had dragged a great cabbage or cauliflower all the way from Misrule's prolific garden, and then said she had just brought it down for Meg to see the funny way the heart curled.

And Meg *would* see, and thankfully, during the two or three dinners which it served and lightened thus her greengrocer's bill.

'Chickie, you mustn't, you really mustn't,' she said this afternoon as she put the things aside. 'The basket is dreadfully heavy, I *can't* allow it.'

'You don't feel a little weight like that a *scrap* on a bicycle,' said the child, so anxious not to hurt that truth was left to go to the wall. And Meg, who had never mounted a wheel in her life, was glad to accept the statement.

'Now I'm off to Baby,' cried the little girl. 'I've been dying for him all the week. He *must* be nearly awake now.'

'If he isn't, don't wake him,' called Meg after her.

'I wouldn't for worlds,' said Poppet, 'the very most I would do would be drop a brick just near.'

Meg put the paste-board and rolling pin on the little pantry table and reached down the flour and baking powder with a light heart; this extra milk would make a delightful plate of scones – Alan loved the scones she made – and now there would be plenty of eggs to go round. She sang 'We are Gentlemen of Japan' in gayest voice as she made her dough.

To her, at the sound of her voice, came Bunty.

'Where's Lizzie?' he said.

'Setting tea,' said Meg. 'Are you getting impatient?'

'She can't overhear?'

'Not a sound – especially if you shut the door.'

Bunty shut the door, moved some crockery aside and sat down on the edge of a shelf.

Meg glanced at him smiling. 'What's she like?' she said. 'Blue eyes or brown? Does she frown on you or favour the suit?'

'It's a long way from a joke, I can tell you,' said Bunty.

Meg looked swiftly grave. Essie, Peter, Esther, Nellie, Pip – all the dear ones she was no longer among, but who were still twined in with all the warm threads of her life – was something wrong with one of these?

'Tell me at once,' she said.

'I hardly know how,' said Bunty, and changed the position of cups that were hanging on a shelf beside him, and took a lid off a teapot and looked in, and spilt the baking powder, and even then had received no help.

'Who is it about?'

'Nellie.'

'Nellie! Why, she was down here as bright and happy as a girl could be on Monday,' said Meg.

'This is Saturday,' said Bunty, with deep pessimism.

'But she was in particularly good spirits,' said Meg, 'and Esther was here yesterday and said nothing.'

'Esther doesn't know – I'm the only one who does, bad luck!' said Bunty. 'It's frightful to have a thing like this on your mind and to feel you'll be a low sneak if you tell anyone, and yet for her good feel you ought.'

'It's something that's come to your knowledge accidentally? Nell would rather you hadn't known?'

'I should smile! She's hardly looked at me all the week 'cause she knows I know.'

'Then you must keep it to yourself. It would be very wrong to tell me,' Meg said.

Bunty looked worried to death. 'Just what I tell myself every day,' he said, 'but she'll get ill. Someone ought to look after her. What can a clumsy fellow like me do? I'll have to tell you, Meg – you never saw anything like how white she is, and she hardly has eaten a thing this week. You'll know what to do – a boy is such a thick-headed ass!'

'Perhaps you had better tell me, then,' said Meg, and floured her scone tin with a very anxious look on her face.

CHAPTER ELEVEN

What Bunty Had to Tell

'What storm is this that tightens all our sail?'

'Well, look here,' said the boy, 'it was this way. You know that chap, Captain Morton, who came to our spree?'

'Yes,' said Meg, and the trouble in her eyes deepened, for she had noticed the gallant Captain's assiduous attentions to her young sister, and been vaguely worried, she knew not why. Since then, however, she had dismissed the matter from her mind, feeling sure that Nellie had too much good sense now to be attracted by a man who, though good-looking enough, was so palpably shallow and insincere.

'What about him?' said Meg.

Bunty's eyes burned. 'He's a bounder, that's what's about him,' he said. 'I'd like to shoot him – no, a gun's too clean for the purpose – I'd like to hand him over to the Boxers and let them finish him.'

Meg bundled her scones on the tin. 'Are you going to

take all day to tell me?' she said, her voice quite sharp with the anxiety. 'Let me know the worst straight off.'

'Keep your hair on,' said Bunty. 'I've got to tell you my own way or not at all. It's the only way you'll understand it.'

'Let me slip these in the oven,' said Meg, and ran to the kitchen for a moment with her tin. 'Now let me have it all.'

'Well, of course I don't know this for certain,' Bunty said, 'but it's my belief the beggar has been making love pretty heavily to old Nellie. At our dance while I was looking after the lanterns I came across them once, and he was holding her hand in a pretty sickening way under a tree.'

Meg frowned. She had conceived the greatest dislike to the man from the moment of her introduction. The older she grew the more and more able she became to find out the people around her who rang true; she might be amused or interested by those who did not, but the only ones she cared to follow up a friendship with were those who, whatever their other faults, had something intrinsically true and high-minded in them. And from the instant she had lifted her quiet eyes to this man's handsome ones she had known the soul that lodged there had not truth in it.

Surely Nellie's eyes, at nineteen, were not blind!

'Well, after that,' continued Bunty, 'I suppose they went on seeing each other a lot. I remember Pip chaffing her about dancing a lot with him at a ball on a man-o'-war. And when she's been to town I've seen him more than once seeing Poppet and her down to the boat. One day when she was alone – I was up on deck – he came right up the river with her.'

'Well,' said Meg sharply, 'it all may have been just accident – Nellie knows plenty of men – she's a pretty girl, they naturally like to talk to her. But she has too much sense to care herself – '

'Oh, has she?' said Bunty. 'That's just where you're fooling yourself. It's my belief you could put all Nellie's sense in your thimble and still be able to wear it. But I thought like you at first – bless your heart, I didn't trouble myself over it. Girls have got to play around a bit – I'll want them to do so myself some day, I suppose – I didn't put my oar in, only to chaff her a bit sometimes, of course.'

'Well?' said Meg.

'Well, I've been busy cramming up for the exam, and then there's the bike – I give you my word I'd forgotten such a chap lived as Morton all this month. The bounder!'

'Well?' said Meg.

'Well, on Monday night you remember it was the tableaux at the Bartholomews'.'

'Yes, Nell came down in the afternoon to borrow those draperies I got in Germany. She was to be "The Lady of Shalott", wasn't she? I haven't seen her since.'

'Yes, something of the sort, hair done any way and a rummy sort of a dress. Well, no one had seemed to think I'd bring down the house as "A Beefeater" or "Henry the Fifth", or anything fancy like that, so I was running the limelights in a little place near the stage – '

'Yes,' said Meg.

'Well, Nellie came in for a second to ask was her hair all right or something, and to tell me to be sure to put the rose-pink light on her.'

'Well?' said Meg once more.

'Well, there was a tableau ready on the stage, only some dook or *aide-de-camp* or someone like that had just come late and was taking his hat off upstairs, and

Mrs Bartholomew told them not to pull the curtain up again till he was ready. So the tableau just had to stand still and wait. It was that chap Morton as Ahasuerus, and Queen Esther was that stunning girl with black eyes staying at the Brownlows'.'

'Yes,' said Meg, and her brows knitted themselves now in anticipation. 'And Nell was in the little room with you all the time?'

'Yes, she hadn't had time to slip out again, she was afraid the curtain would go up just as she ran.'

'Yes.'

'Well, Esther and Ahasuerus began to flirt like any-thing – a good many of the others had done the same – they all must have known there was a chap near working the lights, but, bless you, that didn't stop them. These two went it hot and strong.'

'Yes,' breathed Meg.

'Well, I'd other things to think of, and I didn't want to hear the rot they talked, you bet. And then suddenly I found I *was* hearing it, and they were talking about old Nellie.'

'Yes,' said Meg, her heart a-throb for the other unwilling listener.

'The girl said, "Oh, I don't believe you, you say it to everyone; why, not a month ago you had no eyes for anyone but that light-haired Miss Woolcot".'

'And what did he say?' said Meg.

'The bounder, the cad!' snorted Bunty, 'just smiled in that sickening way of his and said, "Oh, she's not a bad-looking little thing, I have quite an affection for the child. But there is only one Queen – one Esther, and where *she* shines all other lights are only as candles!" And he kissed her about seventeen times.'

'Well,' said Meg, her head up, her cheeks burning, 'what does that matter? Nellie wouldn't care a straw.'

Bunty caught at a cup dangling above his head, and twisted it so savagely the handle snapped off.

'You'd think she wouldn't, but – she did,' he said, his voice grown suddenly thick.

'Are you sure?' murmured Meg. 'What makes you think so?'

'First thing I knew,' said Bunty, 'she got up and went to the door – well, as if she was drunk. I went after her to tell her she couldn't go that way – that it only led out into the laundry. But she pushed me away and would go. Well, I got her a drink, she was as white as chalk – but she couldn't drink it – I was in an awful funk that she'd go in hysterics or something, she was gasping so. Well, that's all.'

It was all the boy could bring himself to put to words; he would not let even his memory go over again the wild two minutes that the girl had clung to him and implored him to take her home, to tell her she was in the middle of some bad dream – to take her home, home.

'What did she do?' Meg said mechanically.

Bunty almost broke another dangling cup.

'Next minute the bell went, and I had to go back to the lights,' he said, 'but I got her to sit down quietly on a tub and promise to wait till I came back to her.' His face lost its look of keen emotion, and a light of most unholy joy came over it. 'I got a bit square,' he said. 'Morton was posing fit to kill you, of course, when the curtain went up, and I mixed up some awful colours, and played such ghastly greens and yellows on his face, there was a yell of laughing all through the room.'

'But Nellie,' cried Meg, her heart torn.

'I was tied fast to the blessed lights for the next ten minutes,' said Bunty, 'and a nice mess I made of them – I didn't know whether I was standing on my head or my heels, and at last they sent two other chaps to do it instead of me – I was spoiling the whole show. Well, I cut down to the laundry and she'd gone. I hunted all over the garden and the verandahs and couldn't find her anywhere. And at last I went into the room to find Pip and get him to come and help me – I thought she must have fainted some-where – and there she was talking and laughing more than I ever saw her in my life, and no end of colour, you'd never have known the least thing was wrong. She's a good plucked one, isn't she?'

Meg had no answer for him, she was dredging, dredging at her paste-board with reckless waste of flour and blinded eyes.

'Even when that outsider Morton went up and spoke to her,' pursued Bunty, 'she answered him just like anyone else. And when she was on the stage she was the best of the whole lot – never saw her look so stunning in my life – everyone clapped their hands off.'

'Isn't it about tea-time?' said Alan, coming in. 'I've been looking everywhere for you. There's been a patient, Meg – seven-and-six, and he'll come again! Scones for tea, eh? Come along, I hope you made enough, or the others won't stand much show of getting any.'

But the scones were burnt to cinders.

CHAPTER TWELVE

The Heart of a Maid

'Out of the day and night
A joy has taken flight.'

The next day saw Meg at Misrule. Every third or fourth
Sunday she and Alan and the baby spent the day there,
leaving Lizzie in charge of the house and the telephone
that too rarely made its harsh music through the hall.

Baby wore something particularly dainty in the shape
of a white muslin pelisse and a white sun-hat. On the boat
people turned again and again to see his sunny little face
and hear his bubbling laughs at the water, the sky, the
smoke that ran out in a grey ribbon behind their progress.

Meg was a little grave and abstracted, her heart heavy
with Nellie's secret. Alan, swift to notice the cloud, had at
first insisted on being told the cause. But Meg had begged
to be allowed to keep it to herself, albeit they gave each
other their frankest confidences always. She explained to
him how it was a little private matter relating to one of 'the
children', and that she had come by the knowledge almost

96

illegitimately herself. So he said, 'Keep it, Girlie', and gave her shoulder a pat, and saw Little Boy did not unduly worry her during the passage on the boat.

At the wharf they were met as usual by various members of the family. Peter had brought his express-cart to beg that the baby might journey up the road in it. Essie had dragged down her large doll's go-cart. 'There's heaps of room in it, Meg, he *couldn't* fall out – oh, do, do, do let me wheel him up in it.'

'I brought my arms,' said Poppet, '*they* won't break down.'

'Anyone can have him as far as I am concerned,' said Alan, mopping his brow with his disengaged hand. 'He's licked half the nap off my hat, and he's tried to walk head downwards down my back, and he's made a concertina of himself and doubled himself up and shot himself out till I'm a wreck. Here you are, anyone – I'll give him away with a pound of tea.'

Meg had stopped to speak a few words to a friend on the wharf, and by the time she overtook her family the 'anyone' had proved to be Peter, who was now careering at a fine pace up the hill, the cart rattling behind him.

Meg's feet found wings.

'How *could* you let him?' she gasped as she flew past Alan.

'He's as safe as a house,' said Alan easily, 'look how high the sides are. The shaking will do his digestion good.'

But Meg snatched her son from the reckless young carter, and Poppet had the happiness of the velvet cheek and the kisses and the surprising weight for the rest of the walk, Essie following enviously behind with her empty perambulator.

Nellie was arranging the flower-vases when they arrived – she did this every second morning, and always threw her heart into the pleasant work, making the daily tables, the mantelpieces and other resting places real feasts for the artistic eye.

Today the mantelpieces showed withered blossoms only, and dead, dry leaves she had not even troubled to remove. For the table, since that duty could hardly be neglected, she was sticking a handful of stiff, ugly dahlias into half-a-dozen vases. She had found these flowers growing a little nearer to the house than anything else.

She looked listless, colourless; her eyes were heavy, the girlish roundness of her face seemed fallen away. Her very clothes seemed to partake of her state of mind – the Nellie whom Misrule had known in a morning was a pleasure to look at, so fresh was her blouse, so exact her collar and tie, so trim her skirt.

This Nellie wore yesterday's blue blouse, and any sort of a skirt, and any sort of a tie.

There were no confidences; perhaps Meg's kiss was a little longer than usual, though unintentionally, for the girl gave her a swift, distrustful look and went back to her flowers as soon as might be. Only when Bunty came in the room did her manner alter at all, and then she talked and laughed about anything or everything in a manner that was absolutely painful in its striving to be careless and natural.

Presently they all went in the garden to superintend the swinging of a hammock in the shade of the trees, that his babyship might breathe sweet air during his day naps. Poppet established herself on the grass close by with a story-book, and a fan to keep the flies off the dimpled face. Esther and Meg strolled about the paths, arm-in-arm, talking, talking. Bunty on the side verandah was seeking for a puncture on one of his tyres, Peter and Essie at his elbow absorbedly watching him try his water-test to that end.

Down at the stable you could see the Major's old helmet, and Pip's cap, and the white tennis-cap for which Alan had been quick to exchange his professional silk hat.

Through the leaves of some low bushes Nell's blue blouse could be seen – she was sitting on the grass, her back against a tree, and a book open in her hand. But Meg, looking at her anxiously from time to time, noticed she never once turned a leaf; just sat there motionless, looking with hard, cold eyes straight in front of her or down on the printed page. Once Meg went to her. Little Boy had awakened up, stretched himself, tossed off his coverlid and held up his warm little arms to signify he was once more ready for the world to take and enjoy him. Meg bore him off over the grass to where that quiet figure in the blue blouse was sitting.

'Would you mind looking after the laddie, Nell?' she said. 'I want to run into the kitchen and warm his food – it is nearly his three-o'clock meal-time.'

Nellie took the child without a word. Any other time she would have jumped up with great eagerness and gone to dance him all over the lawns.

'It's not interrupting you?' said Meg.

'Oh no,' the girl said listlessly.

Meg went towards the house, drawing the reluctant Poppet with her. 'I shall want you to show me where things are kept,' she said. 'I can't be expected to remember Martha's and Bridget's places as well as Lizzie's.'

'Let me go and do it,' said Poppet, 'or let me tell Martha.'

But Meg did not leave to unhallowed hands so immensely important a thing as the mixing of nourishment for so immensely important a person as her son, especially on a summer day like this, when the sun had power to make milk dangerous as dynamite.

When she came back to the garden seat with her tray Nellie's eyes were softer, for Baby was now painstakingly sticking up first one bare pink foot and then the other to be bitten, and now thrusting his curious little fingers into the meshes of her bright hair or trying to insert them in her eyes.

'Here, take your little villain,' she said, a trifle more life in her tone. 'How well he looks, and how sweet in that white frock. I don't feel fit to hold him in this old dress. Take him and I'll run up and change – I didn't go to church with the others this morning, and I'm just as I got up.'

'Oh,' said Poppet in a disappointed tone, 'I did hope we were going to have a really lovely afternoon all to ourselves. Whoever is it coming in at the gate? Let's slip off and hide down near the river, and Martha can say we're not at home.'

But Nell was standing up and also looking through the leafy screen. When she spoke her voice had a metallic sound.

'It is the Brownlows,' she said, 'and Miss Lyttleton who is staying with them. Will you go, Meg? And Esther is about somewhere. I must fly upstairs and change this dress – I didn't know it was so late.'

'Oh, Esther and I will entertain them if you'd rather not bother about changing your dress,' Meg said. 'I dare say they won't stay long.'

The girl who was staying at the Brownlows' – was not this the dark-eyed Queen Esther of Bunty's wretched story? Of course Nell would rather not see her in her present mood.

But the girl's young head was very high. 'I shan't be ten minutes dressing,' she said, and moved hastily to the side verandah steps. 'Poppet, go and see that Martha gets tea nicely ready, will you? I didn't make any little cakes today, but there are wafers and scones. Get a clean tray-cloth, the drawn-thread one, and see Martha doesn't put the old cosy on.'

Meg entrusted the feeding of her Boy to Poppet, and went with Esther to entertain the callers. The men came up from the stables at the same moment, and refused to hear of the womenfolk going indoors. Pip carried chairs and lounges to the favourite corner of the lawn, and eagerly arranged cushions and invited Miss Lyttleton to the most comfortable seat of all. She took it and the young man's homage as a matter of course, and seated herself languidly and yet with a grace that seemed to turn the ordinary pith chair into a royal throne. A dusky, splendid beauty with velvety, magnificent eyes, a creamy skin and vivid lips – Misrule, from the Major to Bunty, and Esther to Essie, found itself waiting upon and admiring her most warmly.

'And where is your other daughter, Major?' the beauty said, 'the one who made such a success the other night as "The Lady of Shalott"? I told Miss Brownlow how much I wanted to meet her.'

The Major looked round. 'Nellie!' he said, 'where is she, Meg? – Peter, Essie – go at once and look for her. She cannot know Miss Lyttleton – and Miss Brownlow – are here.'

Suppose Nell had changed her mind – had found herself unequal to this unexpected ordeal! Meg gave an anxious glance at an upstairs window.

'I am not sure,' she said, 'that she has not gone out – she

was saying something an hour ago about going up to the vicarage to borrow some books.'

But who was this coming down the steps to disprove her words?

Nellie in the very newest gown her wardrobe held, a silky muslin of palest green, made with her own clever fingers in latest style; Nellie with a brilliant smile of welcome on her lips for the callers; Nellie, and on her cheeks a bright colour that had – be the sad secret whispered in shamed tones – been on a rose in her hat five minutes ago.

But those colourless cheeks her glass had shown! Her pride aflame had snatched at the red rose-petal that lay so temptingly at hand and had damped it and rubbed it anxiously, so anxiously on the cheeks where the live rose, till a week ago, had bloomed so freely.

Meg was the only one who detected it; she turned to help Esther with the tea-tray, her throat tightening a little. Presently the Brownlows rose – they had promised to take their beautiful guest on to some friends further along the road. Nell went down to the gate with them, her bright laughter and chatter sounding the most often of anyone's.

Bunty gave a relieved sigh once as he stood near Meg. 'I knew you'd soon fix things up,' he said. 'She's quite herself again, you see, and she's been as glum as a boiled owl all the week.'

But the girl trailed back from the gate as if suddenly tired – nothing the same about her but the gown and the fixed colour.

'Why,' said Poppet, who had joined the group again after a very happy hour with the Baby all to herself – 'I thought that dress was for the garden party at the Thornes', Nellie. Whatever did you put it on just for tea in the garden?'

'Oh, mind your own business,' said Nellie irritably, and picked up a magazine and affected to read it.

'I thought you looked a bit dolled up myself,' Pip said. 'Esther and Meg didn't cut off for their best bibs and tuckers.'

Nellie looked at him coldly. 'Allow me the privilege of managing my own wardrobe,' she said.

Even Esther had a word to say. 'I'd take it off now, if I were you, Nell,' she said. 'It won't look half so fresh on Thursday if you don't. It really is quite a triumph – the prettiest dress you ever had.'

'Oh,' yawned Nellie, 'I don't know that I care to go on Thursday; it is sure to be like all other garden parties.'

Click went the far-off gate again.

'We must have some more tea made,' said Esther; 'that has stood too long. Essie, go and ask Martha to come down for the teapot – she has not brought me the hot-water kettle.'

Four visitors this time, all on horseback. Sybil Moore, small, dainty in a white linen riding-habit, a sailor hat and gossamer; Ralph Moore, her eighteen-year-old brother, whom Nellie's beauty reduced always to a state of semi-idiocy; Edgar Twynam, a plain-faced, quiet-natured cousin of the family, and, riding last of all, Captain Reginald Morton, the 'show' cousin of the family.

Surely Nellie was going through an ordeal of fire this calm Sunday afternoon. Meg's eyes sprang to her; the girl looked quite odd for a moment, so drained of colour were her cheeks – all but those pink patches from the rose-petals. The next minute up came a wave of pink to neck, ears, and forehead.

Bunty crossed the lawn, so clumsily he almost upset the

tea-table. He ranged himself by Nellie's side; you saw his shoulders were squared and could almost fancy his hands were clenched. He scowled heavily at the last horseman.

But Nellie – Nellie of course was herself again by this time. She ran to kiss Sybil, to untie her gossamer, to offer a palm fan; she flung a laughing word to her abject Ralph, another to Twynam, another, just as gay, to Morton.

Bunty drew a breath of relief and sat down. Had he expected Nellie to treat them to an hysterical attack?

Even after Esther's teapot was emptied for a second time, and the seltzogene and fruit syrups had been carried down for the thirsty riders, no one made a move of departure.

The Misrule garden with its face to the river, the cool, soft stretches of shade afforded by the old trees, its flowers, its frank, happy-natured young people, and the absence everywhere of constraint, was the pleasantest place in the neighbourhood on Saturday and Sunday afternoons.

The Major dropped off to sleep on a lounge, a doll's lace cape over his face to keep off the flies. Bunty carried young Moore off to see his neatly mended puncture. Pip bore the dainty Sybil down to the boat shed to see the alterations he had made in the sailing boat, and Nellie strayed about the paths with Edgar Twynam, and was so very sweet and gracious to him and looked so lovely that the level-headed fellow, who in all his thirty-two years had only felt the slightest prickings of the Cupid he had heard so much about, went home with as sharp a dart in his heart as the one that had transfixed young Ralph.

The Captain was left sitting on the grass, exchanging small, very small, talk with Esther and Meg.

His eyes followed Nellie up and down, up and down. He dragged at his magnificent moustache when her merry laughter floated across the grass and flung itself in his face. He had really flattered himself up to a week ago that he had made a great impression on this lovely child, and though not in a state of bondage sufficient to make him cease his attentions to various other beauties he admired, he still felt much chagrin that she seemed heedless of him now. At last Monday's theatricals had she not filled up her programme for the dance that followed entirely without reference to him? She had said lightly, when he reproached her, that she was sorry she had no space, but there were so many very old friends there that night.

There had been a moonlight picnic on the Thursday evening, and she had managed to make herself quite unapproachable to him, kept a shy girlfriend beside her half the time, and for the rest of the time joined the circle that was singing round the bush-fire in preference to the couples who were sauntering about in the moonlight.

And this afternoon here she was giving the whole of her attention to Twynam, and entirely ignoring himself.

He forced an opportunity to speak to her alone just before he left.

'Have I done anything to offend you, Nellie?' he whispered, and bent his handsome, reproachful eyes on her.

Nell looked up at him with quiet dignity.

'Yes,' she said, 'you offend me by that use of my Christian name. It is a familiarity I only allow to old friends.'

He looked at her narrowly. 'I thought,' he said, 'I fancied we were becoming very good friends.'

'Did you?' said Nellie politely.

'Have you forgotten,' his voice was lower still, 'you gave me four dances not six weeks ago – and we sat out one, here in this very garden? And yet on Monday you would give me none.'

Nellie looked at him quietly. 'Perhaps I had begun to see,' she said, 'that you were incapable of understanding that giving you four dances was not a licence to treat me with disrespect. Now I must go, I see Sybil is mounting.'

The Captain stared at her a moment, but he had neither brains enough nor good feeling enough really to feel the snub, and when she moved away, lightly, brightly to the group on the path, he followed perforce, shook hands all round, and rode away down the uneven path, his magnificence in no way dimmed.

But after they had all gone, the red patches stood out on white cheeks again, and the green-clad figure crossed into the house as if suddenly wearied with hard dancing or riding. She did not even come down to tea – said the afternoon sun had made her head ache. The decisive battles might be over, but guerilla warfare would trouble the young General in all weak spots for many a day to come.

CHAPTER THIRTEEN

Holiday! Holiday!

'O frabjous day! "Callooh! Callay!"
He chortled in his joy.'

'Peter,' shrieked Essie's excited voice, 'Peter, Peter – quick, quick – '

'What?' said the perfectly unemotional voice of Peter. He was sitting on the edge of the side verandah and did not move an inch.

'Hurry,' screamed Essie, 'oh, lovely, lovely!'

'What's the good of anything?' was Peter's answer, and he remained seated, kicking the toe of one of his house-shoes against a stump in the path. A hole had already appeared in the leather of the left shoe, and he watched it enlarging with a vicious kind of pleasure.

'Oh, *Peter*,' shouted Essie.

Peter rose up and moved moodily towards the spot where, in a small depression in the first paddock, Essie's blue galatea frock and mushroom hat were to be seen moving about excitedly.

'Bullyfrogs,' she shouted joyously as Peter approached. 'I found them, you didn't. I knewed they'd come back. Had you forgetted it rained last night?'

Peter was investigating with his hand in the little pond of water that always formed in this spot after rain. His heaviness of spirit lightened a little as he knelt on the muddy edge of the depression and felt cautiously about. It was two months since a drop of rain had fallen, and he had actually forgotten there were such pleasant things in life as tadpoles.

'Look out,' said Essie, 'you're getting your knicklebockles all muddied.'

She herself, with the daintier instinct of her sex, was merely standing on a wet stone and prodding the mud of the pool with a stick.

'Let's get the bottle,' she suggested joyously. 'Le's start another 'quarium – the old goldfish bowl, it's not much broked – put my pinky shells at the bottom, ferny leaves all round, the bullies swimming all about – oh, come on, Peter.'

Peter stood up and gloomily surveyed his mud-patched knees.

'What's the good of anything?' he growled. Essie with an effort brought her eager thoughts from the tadpoles to the dejected mood of her brother.

'Oh,' she said comfortingly, 'it's only 'bout eight o'clock, we've only just had breakfus. It's long as long to school yet.'

Peter refused consolation. 'It's always the way,' he said wretchedly. 'Just as you get doing anything you like, that ole bell goes and rings.'

'We don't always hear it,' Essie suggested hopefully. 'If we went down at the bottom of the paddock then we couldn't possibly. Come on.'

Peter remained motionless and miserable. 'She'd only come and look for us,' he said.

Essie's spirits were incapable of being damped. 'Le's ask Mum for a holiday,' she said, and leapt from her stone to dry ground. 'Come on, p'raps she will.'

Peter shook his head in mute misery. Had he not already proffered the petition to his hard-hearted mother and been refused?

'Le's ask Nellie to ask her,' said Essie, 'to beg an' beg an' beg. Come on.'

Peter shook his head again. He had already vainly approached Nellie on the subject.

'P'raps Miss Burton's aunt'll fall downstairs again, and she'll have to stay at home,' suggested the dauntless Essie.

Peter had already weighed the chances of this contingency again arising, and decided against the probability of it.

'Nothing'll keep her away,' he groaned.

'P'raps there'll be nice things to do,' said Essie, who, left to herself, would actually have enjoyed lessons, ' – sums with marbles or apples in, or in the reading-book 'bout "it was the schooler Hesp'rus what sailed the wintled sea".'

'I hate sums with marbles or apples in,' said the comfirmed pessimist, 'and 'bout Casabianca or that Hesp'rus girl makes me feel as sick as anything.'

'P'raps you feel ill now,' said the little sister hopefully.

'It's no good,' said Peter, and wiped his eyes with his sleeve. 'I feel awfully ill, and mother won't let me not go.' A great sob lifted his chest. 'I believe she's stopping loving me, she doesn't care a bit how bad I feel.'

Essie regarded him anxiously. 'Have you got a pain anywhere?' she asked.

Peter gave another sob. 'I've got one all over me,' he said, 'an' I told her about it an' she didn't care one bit. I might be getting plague – I saw a rat in the stable yes'day, truly. P'raps I'll die, and then she'll be sorry.'

Essie laid down her wet stick. 'Le's run an' tell her,' she said, and started away up to the house. 'Come on, p'raps she thought it wasn't a very really pain – le's go an' tell her you're crying.' She ran on over the damp paddock grass, through the hole in the fence, up the path, and burst into the breakfast-room.

Peter followed her, weeping copiously now as he ran.

'Why, sweetheart!' said Esther, 'what *is* the matter? Come and tell me all about it.'

'He feels *so* ill,' said Essie, and burst into tears also. 'He's been crying dreadfully. He might be getting plague.'

'What nonsense!' said Esther, but she looked a trifle startled, for the daily paper she had just laid down was full of this horror. 'What d'you know about the plague?'

'There was a r-r-rat in the stable yesterday,' sobbed Peter.

'A great big r-r-rat,' sobbed Essie.

'You are not to play near the stable,' said Esther sharply. 'I forbid you to go in.' Her frightened thoughts flew to the bags of horse-feed, then to the place where they had come from – those dreadful wharves of the harbour. She drew Peter to her. 'Put out your tongue,' she said.

Peter displayed half-an-inch of it. 'You can't t-tell by just looking at your t-tongue,' he sobbed.

Esther felt him anxiously. 'He's as cool as possible,' she said to Nellie, who just then came in. 'Not the least bit feverish.'

'I think he's school-feverish,' laughed Nell. 'Isn't that it, Peterkin?'

Peter gave a fresh indignant sob. 'I f-feel as ill as anything,' he said.

Essie redoubled her sobs. 'He feels as ill as *anything*,' she said.

Then Esther laughed – for the moment she had forgotten how she had already been entreated for a holiday. 'You little scamps,' she said, and caught her boy up in one arm and her girl in another and cuddled them up to her. 'You bad little scamps!'

But they still wept grievously, for Peter had no doubt in the world that he did feel very bad indeed, and Essie was equally convinced that his condition was really serious.

Esther's eyes went to the window and out to the grass. Such a glory of sunshine everywhere, young leaves fluttering out on the trees, young grass pushing up emerald shoots among the duller blades, dancing lights all over the blue river – a puppy or two yelping on the paths with sheer delight at living, a kitten or two careering in giddy circles on the lawn.

Esther moved out of earshot of the children and looked shamefacedly at Nellie.

'It is certainly a particularly lovely morning,' she said.

'Yes, isn't it,' said Nellie listlessly.

'And I must say I am a great believer in fresh air for children.' Esther had the grace to blush a little.

'It is an excellent thing, undoubtedly,' said Nell, a smile flickering up to the corners of her mouth.

'Your father thought Essie was looking a little pale the other day.'

'Yes,' said Nellie. 'At least I remember he said Peter was so very brown and rosy, that Essie's merely pink cheeks looked almost pale in contrast.'

'Well, that's the same thing,' said Esther unblushingly.

'Oh, exactly,' said Nell.

'It isn't as if they were old enough for it to matter losing their lessons occasionally,' Esther continued. 'Essie is only five.'

'Only five,' assented Nell.

'It is far better for both to be running about in the sunshine, especially as I gave Poppet a holiday to go to Meg's.'

'Far better,' said Nell, 'and think how poor Miss Burton will enjoy a day off.'

Esther's face fell a little. The Major was called upon to pay thirty pounds a year for the morning services of Miss Burton, and just how often that young lady arrived at Misrule door, and was bidden 'holiday-make today,' no one would have liked to tell him.

'It shall be the *very* last time,' said Esther, then she raised her voice. 'Children, you may have holiday this morning, but never, never again – it is the very last time, so it will be no use ever asking me again. Out you run to play – unless Peter would rather I put him back to bed.'

Peter's fair little face shone like a cherub's through its stream of tears. 'I think I feel a little better,' he said.

'He thinks he feels a little better,' said Essie beamingly.

'Then be off,' said Esther, and with a sound very like the puppies' yelps of delight the two sprang away through the long window and rushed out of sight.

'I'm afraid I'm not fit to be the mother of a family,' Esther said, and for the space of ten minutes, while she gave the orders for the day, had an uncomfortable sense of wrong-doing.

Away at the fence that divided Misrule's wild grounds

from the sunless stretches of the pine-surrounded house, Peter gave a low, far-carrying whistle that speedily brought Jack out from his house.

'Hello,' he said, and displayed just one quarter of a glad smile of welcome through the hole in the fence, 'hello – how'd you get out? – Won't they be after you?'

Two eager noses poked through the opening to answer him. 'Holiday – holiday – hurrah, a holiday, do just what they liked!'

The quarter of a smile faded into an expression of keen envy.

'And you had one last week too,' said the little dweller among the pines, 'and I had to do penins'lars and gulfs all the time. I *never* get holidays.'

'Why don't you ask?' said Peter. 'Don't you ever get a pain or anything?'

But the lady of the Pines was not an Esther, and her son knew he might as well save his breath.

'I've got to learn dates and Stephen and John before she comes back,' he said groaningly.

Sympathy passed through the hole.

'Has she gone out in the Box yet?' said Essie. This was the time, she knew, for one of the day's two drives.

'Um,' said the boy.

'Will she be a good long time?' said Peter cautiously.

'Only just gone,' said Jack.

'Tell you,' said Peter, 'me and Essie'll get over the fence and have a look round at your place.' The bold suggestion made him thrill even as he made it, but an extra special holiday like this really demanded extra special doings.

The quarter of Jack's mouth that was exposed to view looked doubtful.

'P'raps you'd better not,' he said. 'Tell you, I might pop over to you for a minute - 1066 to 1087, 1082 to 1100 – Magna Charta, what-d'ye-call it Riots - think I know it enough.'

'All right,' said Peter, a little disappointedly.

But Essie was also carried off the plane of every day by the thought of this extra holiday a-stretch before them. She poked her toes into two knot-holes on the fence and clambered up it, clinging like a tenacious beetle to the top. 'You've been in here 'bout fourteen 'leven times,' she said. 'We won't let you over again 'cept you let us come in your place first, will we, Peter?'

'No, we won't,' said Peter, fired once more. 'We've showed you all our things – the new tap in the bathroom, and mother's pink ball-slippers and everything, and we've let you have tries with the bicycle pumps – now you'll have to let us come over to you.'

Jack looked hesitatingly behind him at his own house. 'What's the good?' he said. 'It's whips nicer in your place.'

'Come on, Peter,' said Essie, who had not scratched her little legs on the rough fence for nothing, 'I'm going – come on, he'll have to let us 'cause it's our turn.'

The dread mother of the house with Lylie was safely out of the way in her Box - one of the men was driving it, one could just be seen mending the hinge of the distant gate – the father was away in the country; there only remained the boy Charlie in all the mysterious place. Peter's courage and curiosity rose, there might never be another such chance.

He swarmed up after Essie, and they lowered themselves carefully and stood their ground firmly.

'Now,' said Essie to her distinctly-dismayed host, 'come on, you've got to show us *everything*.'

She stalked towards the quiet grey house, Peter following a trifle more cautiously, and Jack most unwillingly bringing up the rear.

CHAPTER FOURTEEN

Over the Fence Again

'Heroic deeds will be done today.'

The hall door was closed, but then so too occasionally was that of Misrule. 'We can easily go in the back door,' said Essie.

Jack was beginning to make the best of a bad bargain. 'There's the dining room window open,' he said, 'then Charlie won't see us, he's peeling potatoes in the kitchen.'

Essie's courage rose still higher; this could not be so very mysterious a place after all if homely potatoes were partaken of in it, just as at Misrule.

'Come on,' she said.

Jack pushed open the French window of the dining room, and his eager, staring comrades stepped inside.

Just an ordinary dining room, very well and comfortably furnished, but nothing in the least out of the common run of dining rooms.

'Where's your drawing room?' said Essie.

116

'We haven't got one – we draw in the nursery,' answered Jack.

'Where's your breakfast-room?' said Essie.

Jack led them into another very comfortable room.

'Is this where your father has his meals by himself?' said Peter. He knew there was something rather funny about this.

Jack answered that it was.

'Is this the chair he sits on?' demanded Essie.

'Yes,' said Jack, and the children examined the chair with interest, but found it merely an ordinary chair, not in the least stimulating.

They went out thirstily into the hall, and Peter was interested in the fastening of the front door, which had a chain and ball on a different principle from the Misrule one.

Essie counted the umbrellas and recognised some things hanging on the walls as boomerangs – had they not a big collection of these up at Yarrahappini?

But what terrifying sound was this that came to smite the ears of all the three? Nothing less than the Box stopping at the door, nothing less than the door-gong sounding through the house.

Heavy velvet curtains hung over the hall window and reached to the ground. Quick as thought Jack pushed his comrades behind the folds of them and sat down himself on a hall chair and began saying aloud, 'William the First, 1066 to 1100; Stephen, 1100 to 1035; William the Third – '

He affected to be startled when Charlie opened the door and his mother walked in again.

'Why, you've only just gone!' he exclaimed.

117

'I came back for another wrap,' she said. 'Why are you not in my sitting-room, sir?'

'Lylie buzzes about so a fellow can't learn in there,' he said. 'It's much quieter here – William the First, 1066 to 1077; William the Second, 1077 to 1100; John, 1100 to 1195; Elizabeth, 1195 to 1403 – I'll know it in a jiffy if I sit here.'

'Go back to the chair I left you in,' his mother said, and Peter, who always said, 'But why?' or 'What for?' or 'In a minute', to commands (issued by Esther or the girls, be it understood, not by the Major), knew he would not have dreamed of gainsaying this speaker.

From behind the stifling curtains they could hear their comrade's steps going further and further away, down the hall, up the stairs, till the last sound died away.

Cut off in this alarming manner, Peter and Essie could only cling to each other and tremble.

But that was the sound of the hall door being opened again. 'I shall not be back for an hour at least, Charlie,' Mrs Saville said. 'See that the children stay safely in the sitting-room all the time. Master Jack would not have been downstairs if you had been attending to your duty.'

Charlie was heard to begin a sentence with 'potatoes' in it, but Mrs Saville never heard excuses.

Essie and Peter, beginning to breathe again at a prospect of freedom, let their eyes peep through the lead-lighted hall window. The box was drawn up at the foot of the steps; on top Tairoa sat, idly flicking his whip as he waited. Leaning out was Lylie, her golden hair hanging over her shoulders. Essie's eyes devoured her – white silk frock, white felt hat, gold bird brooch at her neck – what a story for Poppet's thirsty ears! But when Mrs Saville stepped into the carriage again and tried to put on the wrap, the child shook her shoulders, pulled away, and carried on as naughtily as Essie herself did when Martha wanted to dress her in a stiffly-starched, prickling muslin just when she was enjoying making sand-pies. Poppet would never credit this, though Pip might – Pip, who declared that one morning he had seen Poppet's saintly Lylie throw four teacups one after the other out of an upstairs window.

The next moment Tairoa flicked his whip in a business-like manner, and horses, brougham and all vanished away.

Essie was for plunging out of the suffocating curtain instantly, but Peter remembered there was still Charlie to be reckoned with. But Charlie – happy, careless Island boy – strolled back to the kitchen, finished his potatoes, then stretched himself out in the sun at the back door to enjoy a cigarette.

Jack had been able to count on this, and came down now to the release of his friends. They looked a little white and shaken after the experience. 'We'll be going now,' said Peter, and moved promptly to the hall door.

But Jack, with nothing but William the First, William the Second, Henry the First, and Stephen a-stretch before him, was loath to be left.

'You may as well stay now you're here,' he said. 'Come on, and I'll show you how our shower-bath works – it's not like yours.'

'The blackfellow,' said Peter fearfully.

Jack stuck his hands in his pockets. 'If I give him sixpence for 'bacca he won't let on to her,' he said, 'but walk quietly – I've only got ninepence left altogether – I'm always having to give them sixpences not to tell. Tairoa's

119

the best, he'll do it for threepence unless it's very bad. Had to give him a shilling the time I climbed on the roof.'

Peter looked at him with a little awe, then his eyes went hesitatingly to the front door again. It would be very delightful to be on their own side of the fence again, but then there was no knowing how interesting that shower-bath might be.

Essie decided the matter by going upstairs very silently. 'But we won't stay long,' even she said.

On the first landing there was a door ajar.

'That's only the room we do our lessons in,' said Jack, 'there's nothing to see in it. Come on up to the bath room.'

Peter followed him. Essie poked her inquisitive little nose into the lesson-room, and there, at the table, books spread in neat little piles around her, an atlas propped up in front of her, was Lylie, patiently engaged upon an outline of a map of Asia.

Essie rounded her eyes at her.

'Why . . . ' she said, 'why . . . you were out . . . I saw you going out.'

'Oh,' said Lylie, 'mamma will be so angry. Oh how did you get in our house?'

'Jack brought us,' said Essie. 'Why, you were leaning out of the Box. Did you get out at the gate? Did you run back? Why, you've got a different frock on.'

'Jack,' called Lylie, real distress in her voice. 'Jack.'

Jack returned; Peter followed close behind and stared mightily at Lylie, but accepted the odd vision of her and asked no questions.

'Are you going to let on?' demanded Jack of his sister. 'We're not doing any harm, and they wouldn't not come.

They only want to see our bath room tap. If you let on, I'll run away to sea.'

Of course the poor little mouse wasn't going to tell. Jack never had any fear of her when he had threatened her with going down to the sea in ships.

'You – you won't know your lessons,' was all she said.

'My troubles!' said Jack, his valiant front on for his visitors.

'You were in the Box,' persisted Essie, 'you were. You couldn't have gotted back as quick as this. Oh, oh – how *did* you get back as quick as this?'

'That's my desk – that lot's my books,' said Jack, displaying.

Peter looked at the beautiful little desk that had been bought to help to make study pleasant for his friend. He turned over the books, '*Little Arthur's History* – same as us; *Butter's Spelling, Stepping Stones* – 'spose you're not up to Latin, like me – I've gone into the *Principia*. What d'you read out of?'

Jack tossed his books over. 'Where's my *Reader* – have you been hiding it again, Lylie? If you have – '

And Lylie had. Right underneath four or five cushions on the sofa. But she produced it now when bidden, and held it nervously towards him. 'I don't like it being on the table when I'm all alone,' she faltered.

Mrs Saville, in her childhood, had been taught to read out of this same *Reading Without Tears*, and from a certain sentiment connected with the well-worn volume, now taught her own children from it.

But surely we are tenderer of our little children in these days than they were a score or two of years ago, when this same Reader was in the hands of half the young folks

121

seeking or being driven to find a key to the world of books!

'Isn't she a silly?' said Jack, 'frightened at one of the stories. Why, I like it. Here's the picture – look, wolves – they're going to crunch her up.'

'Don't!' screamed Lylie, 'don't!' She put her fingers in her ears, and ran across the room.

Of course Peter said, 'Tell us' instantly, and Essie pressed to listen and see the picture.

'Look,' said Jack, 'that's the girl, only you can't see much of her, she's just going to get eaten. It's about a girl and a little boy, and they lived in Russia or somewhere. And the girl was making bread or something, and the father and mother had gone out. And the wolves smelt the bread, and they came and pushed and pushed at the door.'

'Don't!' screamed Lylie.

'Go on,' said Peter.

"And they pushed the door open, and the girl didn't know what to do, and there was only room for one in the clock-cupboard. So she catched hold of her little brother and put him in it. And when he was in it, he could hear the wolves fighting all over the kitchen, and making an awful row, and crunching up his sister's bones.'

No one would ever know how this story haunted Lylie's sleeping and waking moments.

Essie shivered at it a moment, then she returned to her charge. 'You *were* in the Box,' she said, 'you were. I sawed you. How'd you come back?'

But Lylie shook off the horrible story and ran round to her.

'Oh,' she said, 'p'raps mamma won't mind very, very much. Oh, play you're my little girl, will you? Pretend I have to dress you, and do your hair, and take you out. Oh, I never, never have any one to play with – be my little girl, won't you?'

And for half-an-hour, while the boys roamed over the house, Essie had to submit to be dressed up in shawls and dolls' bonnets and towels, and anything that came handy, and to let Lylie try to lift and stagger about with her, and kiss her and call her 'Little Poppet'.

Nothing would induce either of the trespassers, however, to stay longer than half-an-hour, even though Lylie wept at Essie going, and Jack was so disconsolate, he offered to turn on the gas water-heater, a severely forbidden thing, for the amusement of his visitor.

But the little pair departed as they had come, over the fence, and in perfect safety.

On their own territory, however, something struck them, and they looked at each other in deepest disappointment.

'Why, we never found a thing out!' they said.

CHAPTER FIFTEEN

From the Window

*'A little since and I was glad, and now
I never shall be glad or sad again.'*

A cold, blustering day. Misrule's trees tossed their branches
restlessly, the grass was strewn with dead leaves and blown
rose-petals, the river was silver-grey and ruffled all over with
vexed little waves. Overhead stretched a dull sky with
scudding clouds.

Esther had gone to town, and reluctantly enough when
she looked at the wind, but she had an appointment with
the photographer that might not be put off. Mrs Hassal's
birthday was approaching, and a large counterfeit present-
ment of her small grandchildren was to be Esther's present.
So Peter was inducted into his short fawn overcoat over
his best sailor suit, and adjured to pull up his high socks
and attend to the neat lacing of his best boots. And over
Essie's white muslin was put her warm pelisse of white
velveteen and fur, and on her feet white shoes and socks,
and a white furry bonnet on her brown curls.

Nellie had dressed her and combed out those curls that they might show to best effect in the photograph.

She made a suggestion or two to Esther as she put finishing touches. 'I think I'd only have head and shoulders,' she said ' – the two leaning together, and then have it cut medallion shape.'

Esther looked doubtful. 'It would look nice and artistic,' she said, 'but then you know mother is never satisfied unless she can see all of them, legs and arms and all, so she can judge how they are growing.'

'Tell you,' said Peter – 'Me holding a gun. I could take it with me, Bunty's gun, needn't have any cartridges in – I could be pretending to shoot. Grandma would like that.'

'And me,' said Essie jealously, 'me holding one end of the gun.'

Esther declined the suggestion gently.

'Well, tell you,' said Peter. 'We could pretend to be playing circus – me bending down and Essie standing on my back – that would amuse Grandma a lot.'

'Oh yes, let's,' said Essie, and hopped round the room with one white-shod foot caught in her hand to show her exuberance of admiration at the suggestion.

'Only you always tip over, you're such a duffer,' said Peter.

'I don't,' said Essie indignantly, 'it's your fault, you don't bendle your back down enough.'

'Jack doesn't tip over,' said Peter, 'only silly girls.'

'He does – he would,' said Essie. 'He's a nasty, horrid boy.'

But the bonnet-strings were tied by this, and Peter's sailor cap stuck on, and Esther's lost gloves found, and her purse put in her hand. And down the stairs the three all hastened, and helter-skelter down the drive, and with very little more dignity even on Esther's part down the red road, for had not Poppet rushed from the staircase window shouting that the boat was coming round the bend?

Now the house was settling down quietly once more after the breeze. Bunty went off to the laundry – it was Saturday morning – a tin of metal paste in his hand, to give his bicycle a 'good old clean'. He adjured Poppet to come and do the same by hers.

'In a minute,' said Poppet, who was curled up in the broad window-seat of the drawing-room with *The Daisy Chain*.

'You will do no such thing,' said Nellie. 'Esther said you were to be sure to do your practice. You know Miss Burton will be here at twelve to give you that music lesson you missed.'

'Oh bother,' said Poppet. But she rose up and drifted gradually, reading as she went, to the piano. And here she sat down, put the open book on the music-holder, and played her scales, major and minor and chromatic, one after the other, the while she read absorbedly.

Nell stood at her vacated place in the wide window and looked out at the waving trees and the dull river.

What should she do this morning? Oh yes, of course there was the stocking-bag to be attacked, and the vases wanted doing, and Esther had asked her to label a trayful of bottles of tomato sauce, and Martha would need telling what puddings to make for dinner, since Esther had gone off in a hurry without leaving any orders.

But how dull all these things seemed, dull as the river, the sky, the gum-trees. Oh, what a dull, dull old thing was life altogether – every day the same, getting up and having meals, helping with the young ones, going to little gaieties, or staying at home and reading! Reading – what if she got a book like Poppet? Her mind ran languidly over the books in the house – nothing new. What if she turned Poppet off the music-stool – she would go thankfully – and get out her music? Nothing new there, all the old pieces, old songs.

'A great deal *you* have to grumble at,' said a voice in her heart. 'Think of some girls' lots. You ought to be ashamed of yourself.'

'So I am,' she answered it. 'Still all the same everything *is* deadly dull.'

'You know it's not that,' said the voice, 'all is the same as it always was. It is you who are altering.'

'Well, I suppose it is,' she said. 'I am growing old – I am nineteen.'

'You know it's not that,' said the stern voice, 'the real reason is – '

She shrank from it. 'No, no, don't say it,' she said.

'It is, you'd better face it at once – you've refused to look it in the face for too long. The real reason is – '

'Oh no, no,' she said piteously, 'I've forgotten all about it. If I met him, I shouldn't even change colour – I don't care one atom, one atom. I – I think I absolutely dislike him.'

'Well, why are you letting it change you?'

'Oh, oh,' wildly, 'wouldn't any girl? To have let oneself care, even only a bit, a tiny bit, and to have thought he meant it; but, oh yes, he did look – ah, he shouldn't have looked like that, and held my hand – oh, oh, to think I let him hold it; no I didn't, I didn't, I took it away, I did truly, as soon as I could, or – or almost as soon. And perhaps he imagined I *did* care, and he laughed.'

Over and over the miserable little affair she went. That

127

was the canker, the horrid spot on her sore young spirit. A man had treated her as a plaything, and she had not had sense enough or dignity enough to see it. Instead she had given away unasked – what? Not her heart, that was sound enough yet, but a bundle of girlish emotions and pretty trust and romanticism that she took to be her heart.

She had climbed her stiff bit of hill when she came to it bravely enough, but now she was over the brow of it, and had fought through the thorns no one would ever know how wretchedly flat, stale, and unprofitable stretched out all the level road once more.

What a frightful discord Poppet was making! Left hand and right hand, left so entirely to themselves, had started off on altogether different journeys. Poppet's eyes glanced absorbedly up and down the book in front of her – every minute or two the right hand left its treadmill to flutter a page over and then hastened back to catch up the left as well as might be.

'I ought to stop her,' said the conscience at the window, 'if I were a proper eldest sister – like Meg or girls in books – I should go and take her book away, and sit down beside her and hear her practise properly.'

'Well, why don't you?' said conscience number two.

'Oh, what's the use? she would only argue – I hate arguments.'

'A lazy, self-centred creature, that's what you're growing to be. A love-sick little idiot such as you'd despise in a book. Why can't you brace yourself up a bit and look life in the face again boldly?'

'Love-sick! What a horrible, horrible thing to say! – I'm not, I'm not – he's no more to me than a stone.'

'Well, brace yourself up and stop being cowardly.'

'Poppet, Poppet, put that book away at once – what a thing to do! You are making a frightful jangle. Do practise properly.'

'I am. I'm doing my scales. She told me to practise them ten times each,' said Poppet.

'Not without looking at them.'

'It's good practice, I might be blind some day.'

'Put that book away, Poppet, till this afternoon.'

'Just another chapter – oh, it's dreadful – they've all got scarlet fever, and Leonard is catching it, and – and – '

'What in the world is she doing?' said Nell, an almost startled tone suddenly in her voice.

'What is who doing?'

'Why, Lylie – well, I can hardly believe my eyes.'

The Daisy Chain came tumbling with a crash on the keys, and Poppet sprang across the room to the window where her sister stood. Lylie! Lylie! what could there be connected with her this quiet Saturday morning?

Then her eyes went round as Nellie's, her mouth opened in amaze and forgot to close again.

There was Lylie climbing over the fence and dancing over their grass – the plain, sober grass of Misrule – it was no hallucination. Lylie in a white cashmere frock, with her nimbus of pale gold hair around her head, and no hat on at all. What was she doing now? Walking right on the flower-beds and gathering and dragging at the flowers till her arms were full; throwing the blossoms down and dragging more; pulling the plants up by the roots and flinging them aside; breaking the roses off by their heads and tossing them in the air!

Poppet drew a deep breath and caught at Nellie's sleeve. 'I'm only dreaming, I know,' she muttered,

On and on danced the little white figure. There was Essie's kitten asleep under the marguerite bush, its favourite spot. She caught the trustful little animal up by the tail, swung it up and down, and finally flung it as far as she could in the air, watching it turn over and touch the ground, and creep away dazed and subdued, with peals of laughter.

At the foot of a path was a heap of dried leaves and rubbish that Bunty had raked up to burn, but finding the wind so strong had laid his matches down for a future hour.

The astonished watchers in the window could not see the matches, only the child stooping for a moment over the heap. The next second up shot a pale tongue of flame – the heap caught and crackled.

'Good heavens!' Nell cried sharply, and pushed agitatedly to raise the sash of the long window that she might rush out. 'Her frock will catch.'

Round and round the blaze danced the white figure, moving its arms joyously.

Nellie had the window up now and was dashing out – it only seemed to both of them one minute since they had seen the child climbing across the fence.

Then a scream of frightful horror broke from Poppet. It was no longer a white figure that danced; the pinafore had caught, and blazing from head to foot the child rushed madly across the long stretch of grass shrieking and stretching her arms towards Nellie, who was rushing down to her.

CHAPTER SIXTEEN

Up and Doing

'With a heart for any fate.'

Bunty and the servants ran to the front of the house at the first frantic screams. And Bunty's impulse was the same as Nellie's – to rush to help and never stay to find means. He had not even his coat to help him. The next second he swung round and darted back. 'Blankets, rugs,' he shouted; tore up the hall rug and flew out with it.

Nellie – what was Nellie doing?

'Fool!' she had muttered to herself. 'Fool I was not to catch up a blanket!' Yet on she ran, darting lightnings of thought rushing through her brain. It meant mutilation at least, loss of all her beauty; but oh the child's face of mad, piteous terror, her heart-rending shrieks; she must do something – fling her down, try to roll the flames out!

But what was this! Almost as she reached the blazing figure she stumbled over something, a long black sinuous thing on the grass. Heaven be praised, Bunty had used the

131

garden hose yesterday and left it carelessly flung down on the grass; a trickle of water still ran from it, he had not even turned the water off properly. And now she had caught up the end and turned away from the terrible rushing figure that had touched her, turned and began to run again; her own sleeve had caught, yes, yes, press it out – how easily it yielded to her other hand!

'Don't touch her – don't touch her. You can't save her,' Bunty had shouted as he tore back for his rug. Better that one, a stranger, should perish than that Nell should madly fling away her young life like that.

But Nellie was bending down, bending at the stand-pipe – the next second they knew why she had turned. Out from the end of her hose burst the stream of saving water! She stepped back as the child advanced on her, and played her hose on the pale flames with steady capable hands.

'Lie down, lie down at once,' she called, and the child fell in a heap, and you heard the splutters and hisses of the flames as they went out.

It was all over when Bunty and the servants with their rugs got down. The whole thing had not occupied two minutes; two more waiting for those rugs and the child's life would have been lost.

As it was her condition was alarming. She lay a pitiful little blackened, drenched figure at their feet; all the gold hair burnt away, her face scorched, the white frock, fortunately a thick one, burnt right away, her under-petticoats singed, and her arms in terrible condition. Nellie's face was sheet-white, but she was not even trembling, her nerves were up to highest tension point, and she kept them there.

'Bunty, a doctor,' she said. 'Poppet, go next door and

tell them. Martha, help me to carry her to the house – give me those blankets to wrap her in.'

They bore the shivering, moaning figure up over the grass and into the drawing-room, and by that time Poppet was back again with Mr Saville, the only one at home next door.

The man came up to the sofa with a face like ashes.

'I had fallen asleep – God forgive me, I had fallen asleep,' he said, again and again and again.

'Yes,' said Nellie gently, 'but what shall we do? We must do something, the doctor will be some time – what shall we do?'

'Fallen asleep,' repeated the man, 'and she had left me in charge. God forgive me, for she never will.'

Nellie plucked at his sleeve. 'Think what we can do,' she said, 'that is the first thing. Oh, look at her – listen to her – what can we do?' For a second she had let her nerves relax, thinking here was someone to take the responsibility.

But the poor stunned fellow did nothing but mutter that he had fallen asleep, fallen asleep when he should have kept guard.

Martha came staggering in with a bath of cold water. 'Lay the poor lamb in this,' she said.

Bridget was voluble. 'Mashed potatoes,' she said, 'that is the best thing, spread it over the burns – only there are no potatoes cooked. Will I be after cooking some?'

But Nellie was ready to take charge again. 'Get me flour,' she said. 'No, wait.' What was it Esther used for all the cuts and bruises and little burns in the household? Yes, boracic powder – they must run no risk of poisoning. 'Don't touch her,' she said, and flew up to Esther's medicine-chest two stairs at a time for the familiar red tin. And she dragged a sheet from the bed, thinking of the agony of blanket on that quivering skin. And here was the brandy-flask – yes, a spoonful or two of that.

She pushed the useless father gently aside; she forced the brandy between the white, moaning lips; she cut away gently, very gently, the charred clothing, and sprinkled her boracic thickly on the burns and reddened parts, then laid her sheet on lightly and a blanket over that, for the child shivered and screamed at the touch of the air.

'Now we can do nothing but wait,' she said. 'Martha and Bridget, please go away, I am sure we should keep her quiet. Pull the blind down, Poppet – the light seems to hurt her eyes. Mr Saville, sit where she can see you, will you, please.'

The man obeyed her like a chidden child. 'Here, shall I stand here?' he said.

'That will do nicely,' said poor Nellie, 'and speak to her, poor little thing, try to comfort her – think what pain she is in, and I am a stranger to her.'

He leaned over the sofa. 'Dearie,' he said, 'dearie, don't cry – don't cry, dearie.'

No other sound for nearly an hour in that terrible room. Just the child's moans and screams and the man's dull voice saying again and again, 'Dearie – there, don't cry.' Two or three times when a hand was flung out of its covering Nellie shook more powder on the burns and covered all up again. Two or three times Poppet crept out of the door and up to the staircase window to see if there was any sign yet of the doctor.

The third time she returned her face was brighter and she beckoned Nell to the hall.

'Alan,' she whispered, 'coming down the hill, fast as possible on his bicycle.'

'Thank God!' Nellie said. 'Now if only her mother would come – '

'Nellie,' said Poppet, 'I'm not dreaming, I'm quite awake, but that isn't Lylie.'

'Nonsense,' said Nellie, 'of course she looks different now, that is all.'

'It isn't,' persisted Poppet. 'I knew it wasn't before she caught fire. Lylie is littler and doesn't look quite like that, and her hair isn't quite the same.'

'Nonsense,' said Nellie again, and turned back into the room.

The movements roused Mr Saville from his benumbed state.

'The doctor is almost here,' Nellie said. 'Hush, Lylie – there, darling, the pain will all have gone soon, here is a doctor coming. Mr Saville, can't you get her mother?' She added this in a whisper.

The man stood up and shook as if he were palsied. 'I dare not,' he said, 'I dare not. I dare not. What can I do? Make an end of things?' He muttered the last and turned as if to leave the room.

But Nellie kept her hand on his arm. 'You mustn't leave us,' she said, 'we shall want you. Look, here is the doctor – oh, Alan, at last.'

In five minutes the poor little girl lay perfectly still under the influence of an opiate, the burns were dressed, a folding spring stretcher was carried down and made into a comfortable bed. In this they laid her very gently, and Alan sat down to patiently await the awakening.

He had greatly relieved their anxiety. 'By no means as bad as it might have been, considering the circumstances,' he said. The muslin pinafore had blazed easily,

135

but the thicker cashmere frock had resisted longer, and the body parts were only a little reddened. The arms and legs had suffered the worst, but even these were only injured, as he technically called it, in the second degree. The shock to the system was what he feared the most.

'Did I do anything wrong? – Have I made her worse by what I did?' poor Nellie said, when all was quiet again.

'You did excellently,' he said, 'excellently, everything quite right.' Then he remembered Bunty's hurried account of what the girl had done, and his keen eye noticed the tense look of her young lips.

'Go and get a cup of tea,' he said. 'Remember, it is doctor's orders, no disobeying. I'll stay here and look after the child. And see the father has a cup; he's so unstrung I've not been able to ask him anything yet.'

The father! Nellie had forgotten him for the last few minutes and when she turned to look for him he was nowhere to be found in any of the rooms.

With a catching of breath as she remembered his last muttered words she ran across the grass, scaled the fence almost as quickly as Essie managed to do, and was at the hall door of the gloomy house, as she had calculated she would be, just as soon as he who had gone by both front gates reached it.

'Yes,' he said, 'what do you want?'

He spoke impatiently. Life, long almost intolerable, had suddenly become absolutely so to him. Let him but have a moment or two to leap over the edge of it for ever.

But Nellie was clinging to his arm.

'Oh,' she said, 'I am so faint, will you give me some – some tea?'

The brave girl who had saved his poor little child – and knocked over now, completely spent – what a blind, selfish fellow he had been! He almost carried her into the house, he put her gently into the dining room's easiest chair; then, seeing Charlie and Tairoa had gone to gape and exclaim in Misrule's kitchen, and the coachman was away with the brougham, he busied himself in the unusual and difficult task of making a cup of tea.

CHAPTER SEVENTEEN

A Deeper Sea of Trouble

'With reverent pity as in touching grief
He touched the wounds of Christ.'

When it was ready she drank it thankfully, even though the squatter, with his bushman's ineradicable love of sugar, had sweetened it with generous hand.

For one thing it gave her a little time to quieten her beating heart and think what she best might do, for another her throat was dry and swollen and the excitement had given her a raging thirst.

Then she looked across to her host again and found, now his task was finished, he was standing at the window, his head sunk on his breast, quite oblivious of her again.

She went across to him.

'You must think how much worse it might have been, Mr Saville,' she said. 'Alan – the doctor says there are scores of worse cases continually at the hospital, and they get on very well. She will be well and running about again in no time.'

138

He looked at her piteously. She had never thought of him before as an old man, but now his ruddiness replaced by that grey, curiously-cowed look, his shoulders bowed, his hands shaking, he looked positively aged.

'Oh no,' he said, 'she will die – of course she will die.'

'No, no,' said Nell eagerly. 'Alan says she will do well, he thinks – the shock was worse than the burns – we must just keep her very quiet and take care of her, and you will see how soon she will be well. When her mother comes back she – '

He began to shake again so violently it frightened the girl. Why had she not told Alan or one of them to follow her and help in this dreadful crisis, instead of flying impulsively off alone as she had done?

She took his arm gently and drew him to a chair.

'There,' she said, 'sit down – oh, I know, I know how dreadful you feel, but no one could blame *you* – when she – when Mrs Saville comes home she will quite understand it was no fault of yours. Children cannot be watched every moment – ours are never watched at all – how could you dream she would get into such mischief? It will be hard to tell her, of course, but she can't blame *you*.'

'You don't understand – you don't understand,' he said, 'of course she can blame me – it is the first time she has ever left her for a whole day – since – And she told me not to let her out of my sight one minute. The first time she has gone for more than an hour or two in all these four awful years. She had to go – Lylie's throat has been getting worse, and she has taken her in to a specialist to have some growth removed.'

'Lylie!' repeated Nellie, bewildered. 'You mean Jack, of course.'

'No, Lylie,' he said. 'She took Jack so that he might get into no mischief.'

'But Lylie,' said Nellie again, 'surely that is Lylie at home – Lylie who was – burnt.'

'No, no,' he said, 'that's our poor little Enid – poor, poor little Enid!' Great tears began to trickle down his cheeks.

'We did not know you had two girls,' Nellie said. 'I thought it was Lylie running to me.'

'Enid,' he repeated, 'my poor, poor little Enid. And it was not enough that I had blasted her life once – I do this thing now. Well, well, we'll all go together now – if Heaven had had any mercy it would have finished her off that day at Coorabong, and not let her drag on black year after year to an end like this.' He was talking to himself, Nellie quite forgotten once more.

'Oh hush, hush,' cried Nellie, shrinking with all a young girl's fright from further hearing of tragedy. 'Come back home with me, you ought to be there – don't let us stay here – oh, I want to go home, please, please come with me.'

His head drooped more and more, the mutterings became more indistinct. Nellie only gathered a sentence or two. 'They call it the coward's way – well, let them call it – we'll go together, little Enid and I.'

Her fears increased – what might he not do, left alone in a state of mind like this?

'Oh please, please,' she urged at his elbow, 'oh, do come back home with me, I must go – they will want us both.'

He sat up straighter. 'Well,' he said, 'run along, run along.'

'But you,' said Nellie, 'I want you to come too.'

'No, no,' he said, 'run along – I – I have something to do.' He looked vaguely round the room.

'Perhaps she is crying for you,' said Nellie. 'Think how

terrible for her, no mother there and no father – you *must* come.'

'No,' he said, 'you don't understand. She doesn't know me or care for me now at all – has not done so all these years. But down there – in the dark – she'll remember – and forgive me.'

'Oh,' said Nellie, and her eyes flashed, 'I think it is – not very brave to talk like this. I know it is dreadful, *dreadful* for you. But you are a man, and a man has to be strong and bear things. No one but you can tell her and stand by her – Mrs Saville, I mean.'

'I!' he said, 'anyone but I can. Don't you know it was I who made my poor little girl as she was?'

'I don't know anything,' Nellie said, 'except that you must be brave and meet this – bravely.'

'No,' he answered pitifully, 'not a second time, there's a limit to bearing. I met the thing the first time decently – at all events, I stood it. It's different now. Go back to your home and leave me.' Again he gave that vague look all round his room.

'Mr Saville,' Nellie said, 'I can't and won't go back without you. Don't you think you might do this when I ask you? I – I did my best for your little girl. Look at my arm, I should like the doctor to do something to it.'

The horror came into his eyes as he looked where she bade him and saw the blouse sleeve singed and burnt below the elbow.

'Let us go at once,' he said, 'at once – I did not know you were burnt.'

And in very truth Nell had hardly known herself, and certainly had never stopped to look at the scorched red patch on her white arm.

141

'I *should* like something put on,' she said, and then there were no more words between them all the way down their gloomy drive and up Misrule's sunny one.

The child still lay under the influence of the drug that had been given to her.

Alan was looking for Nellie.

'Have you had that tea yet?' he said, and she just nodded, and pushed Mr Saville gently to a chair by the bedside.

'Mr Saville will watch,' she said. 'I want you to come and do my arm, Alan. It is *so* badly burnt.'

He caught it up in concern, but looked relieved to find it was no serious matter. 'Perhaps it is more painful than it looks,' he said.

'It is dreadful, come and do it at once,' she said, and went before him into the breakfast-room.

But once out of the squatter's sight she forgot the arm again, and hurriedly told Alan of the interview the other side of the fence.

'I am sure if he isn't taken care of he – he will do something to himself,' she concluded, and burst for the first time into excited sobs. 'What can we do? what can we do? and when she comes home it will be worst of all – she is so hard and hateful – oh, you can't imagine – whatever he did she ought to forgive him – who will tell her? – *he* shan't – I will tell her myself first.' Again she sobbed, and shivered.

Alan questioned her about the interview, learned all that Misrule knew of the family next door. It was plain there was some sea of trouble beyond even deeper than this they had just plunged into.

Then he went back to the drawing-room and stood by the bedside again, and watched the father watching his child.

What is the doctor's talisman? The shameful story, the wretched, the sordid one hidden away from the world with such jealous, anxious hands, covered over with such strenuous care, the concealing earth smoothed and planted with gay-looking flowers! And the doctor comes, a man as other men, wise perhaps only in his own way, hardened to suffering, hurried. And down we fall on our knees by the hidden spot, and tear away the fair-seeming flowers, and dig at the kindly-covering earth and drag up the buried thing and hold it naked up to him. Perhaps he only nods from time to time to show he is looking, listening. Yet we are seldom unsatisfied, we know he is sorry for us individually, even though he has looked at just such things scores of times, know he feels for us in the bitter task of the unburying, and that he is going to put forth all his power to work for us.

In ten minutes Alan was in possession of the sad story of next door, and Mr Saville was leaning back in his chair, the relieved look on his face that the mere telling of a trouble often brings.

CHAPTER EIGHTEEN

The Story of the Savilles

'Crying twice, "O child," and thrice
So that men's eyelids thickened with their tears.'

A sad enough tale, in very truth.

The Savilles came from Queensland, where they had owned a big station. Droughts, bad times, the tick pest – nothing seemed to affect them, and they grew richer every year. Mrs Saville had been a lovely, petted society girl, but when the first child came she gave up her gaieties willingly enough, and lived the greater part of the year on the great station, entirely absorbed in her beautiful little girl. After three or four years Lylie came, and later, Jack; but the mother's chief love and pride seemed concentrated on Enid, the one who had come first, and was so bright and lovable, so beautiful and high-spirited that all who saw her were captivated.

Mr Saville shared her pride. It was his delight to teach the little girl to ride, to drive, to swim, and a well-known sight around Coorabong was the pleasant-faced squatter mounted on a big-boned favourite of his, and by his side, on a horse almost as high, Enid in her little holland habit, with a sailor hat and a fly veil, her bright hair blowing behind her, her eyes sparkling, her little hands skilfully guiding her great steed.

When the child was about eight some races were got up among the big stations about, and importance was lent to them by the fact that besides Sydney and Brisbane people a number of English visitors were to be present. Saville himself was greatly interested in the event, and worked hard to make it a success. 'We'll show these English fellows what riding means,' he said, and scoured the country for miles around to be sure no able horseman or promising horse had been overlooked.

There was to be a ladies' jumping contest, and he was anxious to enter Enid for it, for young as she was, she and that loose-boned horse of hers could take a fence with most of the women riders in the district. But Mrs Saville had always been nervous of Enid jumping; indeed it was a matter father and daughter chuckled over and kept to themselves that the latter could jump at all. A born little horsewoman, the child had given her father no peace until he allowed her to follow him over his fences, and at last he had a low hurdle or two put up for her in a far paddock, and took her there to practise daily until she became unusually expert. Utterly fearless himself with horses, he had taught Enid to be the same, and though he selected her horse with the greatest care and gave some hundred and twenty guineas for it, he had little more apprehension for her safety when he watched her galloping beside him than he had for her when he saw her walking about on her own two legs. She entreated him to enter her for the jumping contest. 'Let's do it and s'prise mamma,' she begged. 'Let's keep it secret right till the time.' So he smiled and entered her name. It would be easy enough at the time not to let her start if her mother objected strongly, he told himself. In the meantime he took the eager little rider every day to the actual scene of the races to familiarise her with it, and watched her clear the four hurdles – they were not very high – one after the other as easily as he could do it himself.

The race day came, and all the neighbourhood turned out with all its horses, and all its motley assortment of vehicles, and all its babies. Many of the women rode, and any horse, it seemed, that came handy – a heavy farm one in many cases. Habit-skirts were by no means the order of the day, and the English visitors were vastly entertained by the spectacle, common enough at Coorabong but a very circus item to them, of girls riding in ordinary print or cashmere dresses with frills and furbelows, and an old woman of sixty in a brown stuff dress heavily trimmed with beading and steel work, plodding along on the back of a steed that might have been born the same year as herself.

As a rule Mrs Saville herself rode to these events, but this particular day she was watching the events from the box-seat of the drag, with Jack and Lylie and two or three of the many visitors they were entertaining at the time on the station.

When the ladies' jumping contest was announced there rode into the big ring only some half-dozen competitors – two or three girls in fresh blouses, very long serge riding-skirts and sailor hats, a squatter's young wife in a blue cloth habit, up to date, and a natty felt hat, a tall woman wearing a faultlessly-fitting dark-green habit and an immaculate tall silk hat, and looking for all the world as if she were going for a trot on London's Rotten Row. Saville looked dubious when he saw her, for she made a business of these country races, and carried the prizes off everywhere. Enid had at least a chance among the other competitors, but with this one starting there could only be one end to the race.

He decided he would not even cross the grounds to the drag and beg his wife's permission for their child to start, as had been his intention. He had left the asking until the last moment, thinking it likelier that she would consent if she had no time to think it over.

Then into the ring came riding his little girl. The eyes of the whole course were on her instantly – such a picturesque, small figure in the little white linen habit and the little white helmet, beneath which fell the sunny curls. Such a saucy, glowing, happy little face, such eager small hands – one holding the reins, one the gold-mounted riding whip he had given her.

'No, lassie, no, it's no use starting, you'll only be disappointed,' he said. 'Go outside and watch.'

'Ah, no, no – ah, daddie, I must – oh, did she say so? Oh, let us go and beg and beg and beg!' Such a flame of scarlet on her cheeks!

'I haven't asked,' he said, 'but see, Miss Clinch is going to ride – you would stand no chance whatever.'

'Let me try, let me just try,' she urged. 'Oh, I *must* try, I *must* try – Gaylad is *lovely* this morning, he knows he can win everybody and everybody. Oh, make her let me – make her let me!'

The eyes of all the multitude on his little girl – how his heart swelled with pride for her. She could not win, of course, with that woman there, but how good it would be to show those city people, those English fellows, what she could do!

'Beg, *beg*,' she urged, 'and, quick, quick – they'll be starting in 'bout five minutes.'

He half turned from his place – he was acting as one of the judges – to go to the drag. But here was Mrs Saville hurrying across to the ring on foot. What was it they were all saying – her little girl entered for a jumping race? She was quite white when she reached her husband.

'What nonsense is this?' she said sharply. 'They are saying you have put Enid down for this race. Of course it is untrue.'

'Beg, beg, beg,' said Enid, riding round and round them anxiously.

'Won't you consent, dear?' said Saville. 'I have trained her thoroughly myself. She is as safe as a church on Gaylad, you know. I'd like to show them all what she can do.'

'Never, never,' said Mrs Saville. 'How could you! Send her out of the ring at once. How *dare* you without consulting me? How *could* you?' Her very lips were white.

Round and round them rode Enid.

'Oh, let me, darling mamma, let me – oh, I'll be *so* good always, I'll learn to sew, I'll do *anything* – oh, mummie, mummie.'

The first bell rang for the race.

'Send her out to me – get off your horse and come in the drag with me, Enid, at once,' Mrs Saville said. 'Nothing in the world would make me allow you.'

Saville was sorely disappointed, both on his own account and the child's, but his wife had her rights.

'Very well, dear,' he said, 'of course I'm sorry, but since

you feel like that about it she shall not start. You'd better get back now to the drag, you'll see better from there.'

Mrs Saville moved away again, relieved, and hastened back to her seat, the memory of having left Jack on that high seat hurrying her footsteps.

The riders were in a row and waiting.

'No,' said Saville shortly, 'my little girl isn't starting. Ride out, Enid.'

The child gave one more passionate appeal.

'Oh, daddie, daddie, let me,' she said, 'oh, I know I could win her.' Such eyes, such lips all a-tremble, such scarlet in her cheeks! There was the racing fever in all the Savilles' blood – father, grandfather, great-grandfather, all had owned racehorses and run them. Now on Gaylad's back sat one of the same blood fighting with a feeling she had no understanding of, and that seemed only just born in her.

'Oh, daddie!' she said.

Saville choked something out of his throat. It hurt him like a knife to disappoint her so grievously. He reached up a moment and squeezed her little hand, he made her reckless promises – a new horse, a visit to Sydney, any-thing, anything she liked to ask him to make up for this.

'They are waiting, sir,' said a man.

'Ride out, Enid,' Saville said, and the little girl drooped her face, and rode her horse slowly to the fence.

Saville was to start the race. He gave a quick, irritated look at the line of riders – what interest could he take now in any of them? Then he fired his pistol and off went the eager horses.

Over the babble of the crowd rang a woman's scream. Saville sprang forward suddenly, then stopped stock still.

149

There was Enid riding madly after the tearing horses, Enid he had actually seen right at the fence. To the spectators generally, so quick had the whole thing been, it seemed she had started with the others.

They were at the first hurdle; someone's horse grazed it – you heard the clatter of its hoof on the wood! No, not Enid; the brown horse had skimmed it easily and was striding along, fast picking up lost ground.

They were at the second hurdle. Up, up – and over again, like a bird, like a bird! A cheer broke from the crowd, all for the little white figure and the flying curls.

She was past all but the green habit now. Cheer after cheer rose up as she had gained on one after the other – good horsewomen all of them, but where was another horse of Gaylad's strain?

They were at the third hurdle now, and the white-clad rider was over again easily, easily. Saville's heart was thumping with pride and terror. She was leading – see, half-a-head beyond the green habit, half-a-head, three-quarters, why, Gaylad's heels were right in front of the bay horse's head. But now the green habit is gaining again – yes, yes, she has plenty of strength in reserve. She shoots right on in front, and look, look, the little white figure seems to droop a little, to falter! Saville is tearing over the ground on someone's horse, shouting, cheering – 'Up, Enid, up with him – up, darling, up, up!' It is the only way to save her – excited horse, excited rider, he dare not shout to her to stop and risk her pulling up at such a pace. 'Up, my darling – up, girlie, hold him together, up – p – p!' The green habit is over easily, the little white one rises after it – up, up, well enough, but the race is lost, lost. Oh, bitter disappointment, and the little hands, tired and trembling

with the strain, relax, and the green track becomes a blur,
a noise of hoarse waves is in her ears. Gaylad's head is
not coming up again at all – oh, the crash of his heels on
the wood behind her – oh, the sickening thud on the fresh,
spring grass!

'Daddie!' she shrieks, just before the horrible second,
then out go the sun and the trees and a surging darkness,
rent with a woman's frightful scream, falls over her.

If you had spoken of the occurrence in Coorabong two
months afterwards everyone would have told you that the
child had escaped marvellously. 'Not a bone broken – a
shock to the system, of course – nothing more.' You would
also have heard that the Savilles had gone away, taken the
child to England for a change and to help recovery.

Even four years later, though Queensland friends had
seen the Saville names in the shipping lists as returning
from England, the Coorabong homestead still remained
shut up, and the family seemed to have dropped out of
the lives of everyone. No one even knew where they were
actually living. Occasionally Saville was met by old friends,
but he only spoke vaguely of his place of residence, and
said, Yes, Mrs Saville was well and the children were well.

Escaped miraculously? Yes, the little fallen body had
done that, but the bright, active mind! The frenzied mother
for long refused to acknowledge that anything was wrong
when the first shock had passed and the child was about
again looking like herself, but acting so very differently.
Then, when there could be no longer doubt that there was
something seriously wrong, she rushed to England, to
Germany, to France with the child, and the brain specialists
saw her, and some shook their heads and some said that
time might work the cure that they could not.

And years went on – four, five of them, and the condition remained the same – a state of stupor occasionally varied by fits of wilful and malicious mischievousness.

The mother shrank unutterably from the fact being known. She clung tenaciously to what one of the German specialists had said – that at fourteen there might come a change and the torpid condition might pass away. In the meantime she put forth all her powers to hide the present state, lest when the girl was grown up and possibly well again people should whisper and point at her.

The lonely, tree-surrounded house next to Misrule had struck her as the one place where they might live comfortably and healthily and yet hide the secret. She engaged Island boys for the housework to avoid having chattering women-servants, and then with dogged patience she set herself to the work of combating the girl's heavy moods, training, suggesting, watching, watching. Such a task demands the best bodily, mental and moral powers, and they were forthcoming. She became a woman of one idea, interested in nothing beyond the daily development of her unfortunate child. She discharged her duties towards Lylie and Jack most faithfully, taught them herself, to avoid bringing anyone else to the house, even tried to find amusements for them. But she seemed frozen at the heart, and in all those five years she had never forgiven her husband, never spoken an unnecessary word to him.

He acquiesced in the punishment, and became a quiet, gentle fellow such as his old friends would not have known. Though his wife would have little of his help with the child, preferring to rely solely on herself, still he stood by, ever ready, leaving home only when business took him, and hastening back as quickly as might be to the gloomy place, he whose nature seemed made for merriment, sunshine and prosperity.

He would never forgive himself – that went without saying. Never would he lose the memory of that green paddock, and the brown horse with the little white figure as it rose over the fourth hurdle and crashed down the other side.

But in all that time he had never even tried to clear himself from blame to his wife, never told her that he had sent the child out of the ring, and had never dreamed of her starting. He felt he could not lay the blame on the poor little girl's shoulders and tell of her wilful disobedience; the fault was his, for he had taught her to jump, had wanted her to be in the race; the childish impulse that had led her to start her horse when the others did she should not be held accountable for.

And yet had he spoken it would have made some difference to his wife; for the most bitter and the most unforgivable part to her had seemed that after promising her, the moment her back was turned, even before she could take her seat again in her drag, he had gone from his word and permitted the child to ride.

So the dreary years dragged on, and the five lives that had been as full of sunshine as their bright Queensland was, moved now in the deepest shadows.

Lylie grew up curiously like her poor sister in appearance, but timid, shrinking, depressed as was natural. Jack, his father's nature stronger in him, made attempts to enliven his days as has been seen.

Saville spent a fortune on toys for all three of them, and carried the two younger ones off from time to time to the pantomime, to circuses and such, to try to make up for the gloom that was their daily lot. He had begged the mother to allow the companionship of the young ones from Misrule, but she had vehemently refused, not trusting the discretion of either Lylie or Jack until they were older.

'They are better off than many children as it is,' she said coldly. 'They must expect, situated as we are, to make some sacrifice for Enid, who is cut off from everything.'

It was when she took Enid for the daily drives in the brougham that Jack had made hay, though so firmly had even he become impressed with the necessity of telling nothing abut the strange sister who lived upstairs and did such queer things from time to time, that Misrule had never learnt from him that he had any sister but Lylie.

And then a whole day's absence of the mother and here came this new and frightful tragedy!

Saville had been sitting with the child in the beautiful room they had furnished for her, watching her as she sat turning over and over again a box of coloured bits of silks and velvets. She had not grown very tall in all these years, indeed Lylie had almost caught her up, but she looked strong and healthy. The hair was the same, the bright light curls that had blown out in the wind that frightful day. But the eyes that had sparkled and danced, the bright face that had had the young soul aglow in it – ah! these were changed, lustreless, expressionless. Saville had sat watching her in saddest reverie, thinking of the days when she had galloped, laughing, chattering, by his side over the white roads round Coorabong.

And sleep crept over him! The strain of the trouble had made him a victim to insomnia all the five years, and the last two nights had been the worst he had ever experienced.

Outraged nature rebelled, his head fell back against his chair and he slept – slept and dreamed he was lifting his beautiful girl, laughing, loving, up on to Gaylad's back.

And Poppet had awakened him, shaking him by the arm, sobbing, shivering, gasping about the fire.

CHAPTER NINETEEN

Along the Road

Some mile or so from Misrule stood the Moores' house, where dwelt the dainty Sybil whom Pip always placed as central figure in the castle his early manhood's dreams so often built. Here, too, for the last year had made their headquarters two nephews of Mrs Moore: the gallant Captain Reginald Morton, recruiting there on Saturdays and Sundays after his war experiences and living in barracks during the week, and Edgar Twynam, a reserved, quiet-natured man, lately come from England to establish an Australian branch of the great iron works owned by his father and himself in Manchester. This Saturday of the trouble at Misrule he had been spending at home, working through a mass of correspondence to catch the next mail.

But after the one-o'clock lunch he took his pipe to smoke on the road, a new restlessness in his veins compelling him to strike beyond the boundaries of his uncle's well-kept grounds.

It was freer, fresher out here on the open road. The house he had just left was the last one of the suburb, and where its fence ended the untouched bushland began again and ran up and down the gentle rises parallel with the river, until the roofs and fences of the next suburb stretched out to meet it.

And yet it was no day for pleasant strolling – clouds of red dust blew up and down the road, the gum-trees waved wild limbs on either side of him, fragments of clouds whirled like driven smoke across the white sky where now the sun shone and now turned its face away.

He shook himself once or twice; he tried to laugh at himself. Here was he, arrived at the mature age of thirty-two, almost without a single 'attack of the heart'; he, come scatheless through countless moonlight nights of long voyages on ships pervaded by lovely women; he, escaped from the pretty traps laid for him by anxious mothers who had knowledge of the fact that his income was two or three thousand now, and would at the death of his father be trebled.

Here was he swearing to the stars at night that Nellie was the sweetest name on earth; he, superintending the putting up of great ugly buildings, and seeing before him on every wall a girl face with sweetly-fringed eyes and hair aglint with this southern sun; he, going over and over again with deep anxiety what she had said to him, and what he had said to her at this tennis-party at his aunt's, at that meeting on the old riverboat – whether he had said anything foolish, or presumptuous, or in any way different from just what she would have him say.

'I believe it is best to get it over like measles and whooping-cough while you are very young,' he said to himself, as he walked and smoked, realising ruefully how little work he had done that morning, and how often his eyes had gone to the window from where just one chimney-pot of Misrule could be seen through the trees. 'I've got the disease as acutely as poor young Ralph in there, and stand just about as much chance. A bright young thing like that would have nothing to say to an old slow-going fogey like me. If I'd some of Reg's attractions now – !' He sighed and puffed very hard at his pipe, and tried to get up courage to promise himself he would go away – go and put up at some hotel in Sydney while his works were in progress, and stay no longer in this dangerous neighbourhood that every day became dearer and harder to leave.

He swung round at last telling himself fiercely he would go back to his letters and then start and pack up; what chance could he stand, and even if he stood a chance what prospect had he of making her happy? 'I'm a cut-and-dried bachelor – the last man a girl like that would look at,' he muttered, 'and now that's the end of it, so pick up your tent and go. Well, it's really goodbye this time, little Nell.'

And there as he swung round, coming down the hill towards him at an unusually quick pace – even running now and then – was the girl he had just bidden goodbye to.

The Nellie he had shrined in his heart was a particularly dainty little lady, loving fresh, delicately tinted dresses, possessed of a weakness for becoming hats and pretty shoes and gloves.

The Nellie walking towards him wore a very old jacket and a serge skirt that seemed to be wet and draggled at one side. On her roughened hair was stuck, crookedly, a sailor hat. Her face was not even clean, for a black smut had been smeared on it and extended right across one cheek.

He stood stock still and stared at her for a second even before he held his hand out. But she clutched at his sleeve instead.

'Oh,' she said, 'you! Oh, I am so glad it is you – you are always so – so sensible. You will know just what to do.'

She spoke breathlessly from running against the wind. 'I – I was afraid,' she added, with a gasp, 'when I saw you first it was Ralph or someone young. Oh, I am glad it is you.'

'Just so,' he said grimly to himself, 'didn't I tell you so – a regular patriarch to her, that's what you are.'

But the girl swayed for a second, and turned so white that he forgot his own feelings and put a steadying arm around her.

'It's nothing,' she said. 'I was a little giddy, that's all. I've run most of the way.'

'What can I do?' he said. 'You are in trouble – is someone ill, do you need a doctor? I can go quicker than you.'

'No, come with me, that's all,' she said, and started to hurry onwards again.

She told him briefly the events of the morning, and why she was hastening in this manner.

Alan had come to her half-an-hour ago and asked had she the strength left for one more task. Saville had just told him his story, and the young doctor recognised that even less than the quiet figure on the bed might this man be left alone in his present state of mind. Otherwise he had formed a notion of going down the road himself to meet

159

Mrs Saville's brougham, and prepare her for the shock that awaited her.

'Can you do it, Nell?' he asked. 'You are a woman and will manage perhaps better than I. And can you also show her her husband's critical state of mind – the extreme need there is she should meet him without bitter words?'

Far rather would Nellie have met another blazing figure and helped to crush out the flames, but she nodded and reached blindly for an old hat and jacket that hung in the back hall.

'Shall I wait at their gate?' she said.

'No,' said Alan. 'Saville says she must already have started back from town – if you could meet her some distance down the road it would give her longer to prepare.'

So Nellie went down the windy drive and down the red road – slowly at first, and then the memory of that poor father, trembling with terror at the idea of meeting his wife, suddenly gave wings to her feet and she flew along. A mile – two miles – oh, let her meet her as far away as possible to give that stony nature time to soften just a little towards the culprit.

'Oh, if you only knew her,' she said, as she hastened by Twynam's side, 'cold, bitter, hard as rock. I don't believe she has a heart at all. Her husband, her very own husband – whatever he has done she ought to forgive him, oughtn't she? She has hardly spoken to him for five years, he told me so himself and Jack told us. I suppose it must have been something very bad, but still, *still* she ought to have forgiven him. And just think of me having to tell her what he has done, now! Oh, I can't, I can't, I can't.' She began so sob dreadfully, and stopped and looked back as if she would turn and run back over the road she had come.

But Twynam had his hand on her arm, and he drew her to the side of the road and on to a fallen log, and he forgot that he had ever thought of her as his wife, but just felt she was a little trembling girl who had to be helped and comforted as he had often helped his own little school-girl sisters.

'There, don't cry, dear,' he said, 'it has all been too much for you. We are just going to wait here till the carriage comes, and then I am going to break it to her. Will you leave it to me? Believe me, I can manage – don't you see the whole thing is so frightful there can't be much "breaking it gently" to her? She has just got to know, and as quickly as possible, or it will be worse torture to her. And see, here's the station cab coming along, I'm going to keep it. You say her children will be with her – we mustn't frighten them, poor little souls – one delicate too, you say.'

Nellie sobbed less violently, and sat up and looked along the road. Oh, the exquisite relief to have someone here helping her, taking the biggest burden off her shoulders.

'There's something coming along now – yes, it's a brougham, I suppose that is it,' Twynam said, 'not many people about here have them.'

'Yes, that is the Box,' said Nellie faintly.

Nearer it came, nearer, nearer. Twynam put up his hand and signalled the coachman to stop. He stepped to the window, lifted his hat. A dark, haughty, surprised face looked out at him.

'I must speak to you,' he said. 'Will you come out of the carriage, or may I lift your children out? I have something to tell you that they should not hear.'

A frightful look sprang into the woman's eyes, she glanced at him, at Nellie, whom her sharpened senses instantly recognised, then at the little pale face of Lylie leaning against the cushions, and Jack sound asleep in his corner.

'Something has happened,' she said swiftly but very low – Lylie heard no word of her speech. 'Something has happened at my home, my child – what – what? I knew it – something told me hours ago – what is it?'

She was opening the door as she spoke, stepping out, falling to the back of the carriage with this stranger who had, she knew – such was the strange wave that had washed from Enid in her peril to her mother heart – some terrible news for her. Nellie, a few yards away, watched them talking – saw by the deadly whitening of the woman's face the moment the blow fell. And yet he detained her a minute or two; spoke more words in that quiet, strength-giving voice of his; told her how the child's danger was past, the husband's only just beginning – that his life lay in her hands only.

Then they came towards Nellie, and Twynam was leading, helping the woman to walk, tenderly, gently, as if she were his mother, stricken with age and feeble.

'Mrs Saville will go in the cab with you, Miss Woolcot,' he said, 'you can tell her anything she wants to know on the way. I'll follow on with the children – you can trust them to me, Mrs Saville, I always get on well with small ones, and I will invent some story that will satisfy them for the exchange.'

Back, back along the road they drove, the swift fly, the slower following brougham. This the proud, haughty woman with the icy heart that Nellie had felt she could never reach! The strength that had upheld her all these five years and made her coldly self reliant, distrustful, bitter, fell all away from her. She clung to the girl beside her like a helpless child.

And when they dashed up Misrule's drive, and Alan came to the door, and beside him, ashen pallor on his face, the husband, what did she do then?

Tottered towards him, drooped into his arms. 'My husband, my poor, poor boy, help me to bear it,' she said.

Nellie slipped away – Alan went back to his little patient – and there in the hall they clung together, husband and wife who had been apart such years, such frightful years.

Presently they went into the room where the child lay, and the grey had gone from the man's face, and his shoulders were straighter, and he was leading his wife tenderly.

And when they had been standing there by the bedside a little time, the child's eyelids fluttered open, and she stared up with great wide eyes into their faces.

'Was Gaylad hurt, too, daddie?' she whispered.

CHAPTER TWENTY

No More Pine Trees

Life fell back into quiet streams once more, and in a month almost every trace of the storm that had whipped its waters into such a turbulent state had gone. At least, every evil trace; for like the eddying, ever-widening circles that start from a careless stone cast into a quiet pond, the good results went on and on till none might say where they ended.

Enid recovered slowly but surely under Alan's vigilant care. In a month she was about again, one arm only still in wrappings. Happily there was no disfigurement but the loss of the mane of bright curls, and that would soon grow again. She went about strangely, shyly, a pathetic little figure with a boyish, curly little head, and puzzled, inquiring eyes. Where was Gaylad? Where was Coorabong? This seemed a very strange, dull old house. And who were all the nice children always coming in to see her? She could not remember them at all. How funny Lylie looked, why she was nearly as tall as herself! And Jack – Jack had worn little holland jackets – it must be having those knickerbockers on that made him look so old and big!

The mother and father watched her tremblingly, fearfully. They could hardly bear Alan to leave the house, they hung on his every word, they entreated him to take as little time as possible for his other patients – they would be only too thankful to make it up to him, a thousand pounds, two thousand – anything he liked to ask.

How strangely things fall out! During that dark time in Germany, the same great brain specialist Alan had come across was the one on whom Mrs Saville pinned all her faith. The German doctor had conceived the greatest liking for the young Australian one, and had given him priceless opportunities for studying with him his own special-ity – opportunities Alan thankfully embraced as helping him to pass the leaden hours, and furthering him in the profession he loved. When, therefore, Mrs Saville knew Alan had studied under this man, and practised his theories, she was ready to go on her knees to him to undertake the watching of Enid's case; there was no medical man in Sydney she would have trusted as readily.

For though, with the shock, the brain lethargy had been shaken off, the child would need for a year or two great care and watchfulness, for the newly wakening mind had to be strenuously guarded from over-fatigue or over-excitement.

Misrule never learnt the secret; that remained locked for ever in Alan's breast. They were all told of the accident at Coorabong – that much Mrs Saville herself told Nellie and Esther, but they were led to believe the quiet life had been necessary to restore the child to health; that some deformity had been feared, and the thought of it had soured Mrs Saville's nature and made her dislike and dread the approach of anyone from the outside world.

'Yes, just fancy,' said Poppet, 'if her spine had been broken, and she had had to lie on a sofa for always like Alice Humphreys in the book! You can't wonder they were so miserable and had to look after her so carefully.'

None of them had even a suspicion that there had been anything wrong with the child's brain; shy and backward she might be, but in everything else she was just like any of themselves now; even her action in uprooting the plants and lighting the fire they set down to the fact that she must have become very spoilt with being so long ill.

Nellie was obliged to spend half her time next door. Mrs Saville clung to her as if she, young Nell, had been an elder sister. The woman's whole nature seemed to have changed; she was gentle now, and all her cold self-reliance had gone; she leaned on her husband first and after him on Nell, and the leaning made the girl both stronger and more womanly.

It was she who had suggested most of the changes that had already taken place at the gloomy house. The pines had all been chopped ruthlessly down, and the pleased sun did as he liked in the garden – it was as bright as Misrule's now. An architect was called in to cut away verandah roofs where they interfered with the free entrance of the same genial warmth-giver. The place looked quite delightfully commonplace now, and all the air of dark mystery had entirely departed. You might pass the gate and see the squatter smoking happily anywhere about the grounds, his wife close at his side, Enid darting about with Lylie, Jack boldly coming and going through the dividing fence from which several palings had been torn bodily, and whooping and shouting to his heart's content.

You would see Poppet running through the opening to consult with the little girls about Cherry's new winter clothes. Peter, pushing wrathfully through to fight young Jack for something or other; Nellie, bright-faced, singing, going through, her arms full of flowers to arrange in next door's vases.

So full was life for her now, so sweet was it to feel herself of such real use to these people, that she found herself actually laughing out loud one day when, turning over a drawer, she found a portrait of the gallant Reginald that she had once cut out from an illustrated weekly.

'To think I was ever such a little donkey,' she said, and did not even trouble to take him to her candlestick and burn him to grey ash as the slighted heroines in her books always did, but merely crumbled him into a little ball and tossed him out of the window.

And he lay there on the wet grass, neglected for days, till Flibberty-Gibbet, having nothing better to do one day, pretended to worry him for a rat, and stuck his sharp little teeth into the manly breast, and tore off the magnificently moustached mouth, and chewed up the brave helmet.

And that was the end of that little affair.

CHAPTER TWENTY-ONE

A Heat Wave

Baby had been ill – King Baby. He turned his little head aside when they offered him food, he had hardly a smile for Bunty's wildest contortions, he just picked up the toys that Pip still brought him and looked at them and dropped them wearily from his tiny fingers again. He cried very little – everyone would have felt happier if he had been outrageously cross. All he seemed to want was to lie with his head against Meg's circling arm, or with half-shut eyes in his own quiet cradle.

Heat wave had followed heat wave, and as early in the year as November. The city lay sweltering for days at a stretch under a moist hot haze that no breeze came to lift. The advertising columns of the papers were full of 'Mountain Cottages to Let', 'Board and Residence on the Mountains', 'Mountain Breezes for jaded City Folks', 'Accommodation on a Farm: Poultry, Milk, Cream'; and train after train climbed up the rises every day to the pure air, laden with men and women and children hastening away as far as they could from the beautiful harbour they loved to boast about – where heat waves were not.

Alan tried various remedies for his little son; he even prevailed on Meg to take him to Misrule for a week to see if absence from the narrow terrace house would improve him. But the same hot, moist air hung over Misrule too, and still the tiny boy drooped like the wilted flowers in the garden.

'You must take him to the mountains, Meg,' Alan said, the day she came back from higher up the river, and the boy still lay quiet and listless in her arms. Not a movement did he make to go to his father, and only a month or two ago he had begun to double himself up with glee and to fling himself frantically forward the moment he saw Alan. Meg whitened a little – she had hoped he would have thought the child better.

'As soon as his tooth is through he will be quite right,' she said.

'Well, we won't wait – you shall take him away at once,' Alan said. 'Can you pack up and catch the early-morning train?'

It was seven in the evening then.

'Of course I can,' Meg said.

The cost? That had kept them back before when Meg had read the advertisements, and longed to carry her darling out of the heat. But now that must be the last thing to think of, for Baby was more than 'not very well', he was ill – little King Baby.

Alan held his little son while Meg got out a dress-basket and a portmanteau and began to put things in.

'Take enough,' Alan said. 'I'm afraid, dear girl, you must make up your mind to spend the summer there.'

Meg just nodded, and added a few more pinafores and a few more frocks.

For now she knew Alan considered the case to be serious. Her brain worked as well as it could through such anxiety. Money thoughts rose up – how might she do this thing most economically? Things were certainly very much better now with them, for Alan had a 'Lodge' – it worked him to a skeleton, it goes without saying, for its hundred and fifty pounds a year – the Saville cheques were princely and other work was coming in steadily and surely.

But a six hundred-pound debt is a heavy millstone to seek to swim with. The little household still bound itself within the same narrow means; Meg turned and twisted her hats and frocks about, and packing-cases, skilfully concealed, still formed the greater part of the house's furniture. Yet it was great happiness each quarter to add up one column of the ledger and subtract the total from the other column, and find a very large remainder on the right side. Within a twelve month they had paid a hundred back to the Major and a hundred to Mr Courtney, and were well pleased with themselves.

This new expenditure for change away from home would make a big hole in the amount they were putting in the bank for the next quarter's payment. Meg planned and packed, packed and planned. How to leave Alan provided for? He must have his meals carefully attended to, for he was working cruelly hard. And Lizzie, though willing and now – after arduous training – fairly competent, was curiously forgetful and unreliable if left alone.

Help from Misrule? The Major had sent Esther away from

the heat to Yarrahappini with Peter and Essie, and Nellie was managing the Misrule *ménage*. But Poppet! Poppet had started going to school now, a school in Redbank – she would ask for thoughtful little Poppet to come and live in the Terrace, and give the orders for the day, and generally keep Lizzie up to the mark.

Just where to go herself? Every place was crowded with visitors, and the hotels and boarding houses were asking extortionate prices. All they could do was to telegraph now for a room in a hotel at the highest point, and when there to look about at leisure for a more economical place.

And so things resolved themselves gradually into working order. Alan was called out to a tedious case, and Meg continued her preparations far into the night haranguing, and entreating Lizzie, writing lists for her, watching and nursing the poor little baby, packing and thinking of all the things she would require for the next three or four months. Alan came back about two in the morning, weary-eyed and pallid with the long strain of the case he had just left.

And Meg, worn out, broke down for just two minutes.

When he drew her into his arms, away from her packing, and kissed her ruffled hair, and the little worry-frown on her brow, and the tremble on her lips, she drew her breath back sharply and to her dismay found it ended in a sob.

Then she clung to him hard. 'How can I leave you?' she said. 'I can't, I can't.'

A wave of the coming desolation swept over him too, and he held her fast. 'How can I let you go? Mine is the worst – I lose you both!'

'Oh, if you could come too! And you need it badly, badly! I hate that "Lodge". Give it up – you are killing yourself.'

'You are tired, darling, or you wouldn't say that. Where's my brave girl?'

'Gone – gone. I am only a coward – and I love you, love you. It kills me to see you worked so hard.'

'Nonsense, I like it – it is all I asked – plenty of work, and it has come at last. But I've got to grumble a moment at losing my darling for so long.'

'If it were anyone but Little Boy I couldn't go,' said Meg.

'Ah, but it *is* Little Boy.' Alan drew her to the cradle, and the child, waking from his unrefreshing sleep, looked up at them.

Alan lifted him up and held him close. 'Little Mr Son,' he said yearningly, even Meg hardly realised just how this tiny boy stirred all the untried depths of his young father's heart.

The boy gave one of his old tugs at Alan's necktie, and then fastened on to a button of his coat. And the eyes of both father and mother filled with quick, glad tears. It was the first time for so long that he had done as much.

'Be glad to go, dear one,' Alan said.

'Glad!' said Meg, and gathered her baby into her arms and held him close, 'I would go to the world's end with him, my boy, my bird, my little tender bird!'

CHAPTER TWENTY-TWO

Meg on the Mountains

Then was the western mail so much the heavier by reason of the letters going up to Meg's retreat and coming down.

> *Up among the clouds,*
> *November 16th*

Here we are (wrote Meg to Alan), safely arrived and housed and rested. Laddie stood the journey well, though the train was packed, and he drank all his milk when we got here, and even made an attempt to gnaw one of his old favourite biscuits. May I let him eat them, if he will? And shall I still give him the brown medicine?

Dear one, I am ashamed of being a coward. I am 'twite good again. So much was granted to us at Heidelberg I meant never to grow distrustful again

173

all my life. And now I know my tiny darling will grow better fast, and be our own saucy, jolly boy again in no time. And the months will pass, and I shall come back to my sweet, ugly little terrace home again, and we shall all live happily to the end of our days.

It is the living apart – you and I whom God joined together – that has to me such a terrifying aspect, that dulls my heart and makes me unwilling to know the date, and so remind myself how far off is the end of the summer. And yet how babyish that sounds. There is a woman here at the boarding house, quite young yet, and her husband has been two years away in Western Australia! There is a woman here, and her husband has gone to England. There are two or three women here come up for the whole season, and they say, as a matter of course, that they will not see their husbands for months. And none of them seem to think themselves very 'lone lorne critturs'. It won't do, will it, to say like Mrs Gummidge, It is worse for me than any of you, I feel it more?

But, ah, Laddie, Laddie, there never were any two just as much to each other as we are; just as absolutely necessary to each other, were there? I might go without my lover a little time perhaps – only perhaps – but see, I have lost my chum too. If it were only my chum away – but to do without my brother also! And sister and mother yet again. And father of my tender little babe, and doctor to his poor little needs! Did you know you were all of these things – all and more? That is why I feel sure it is worse for me than for these other women, and that I *do* 'feel it more'. I know they have just got plain *husbands*.

Dear one, do write and promise me never to go out in the early morning, or when you come in tired – even to an urgent case – without coffee or something. If Lizzie is not up, you can make it in five minutes yourself on the gas-ring with coffee essence. Or make cocoa, it will be even better. I lie and worry over the thought of you rushing off, when you are tired out, to some horrid infectious case, or else coming back with a chill that will turn into pneumonia. Oh, why, why are you a doctor? Why aren't you a nice respectable grocer or draper, able to put up your shutters on the world at the end of a day, and sit by your fire for the evening, and loafe and invite your soul?

I got the books and magazines safely – you made a lovely selection.

Boy is just waking, so I must take him up. I am sure there is more colour in his cheeks already.

Goodbye, my lover, my own husband, my dear, dear laddie.

Your very own

WIFE

DEAREST NELL,
No, on no account – no, no, no – I am managing splendidly. All the same, thank father very, very much for offering to lend you to me. I quite realise the amount of domestic discomfort he was ready to expose himself to to part with you while Esther is still away. Of course I got away from the hotel as

soon as possible – it was three guineas a week! I am only paying twenty-five shillings where I am, and it is quite comfortable. You can guess the kind of place, for you have been up here – a weatherboard cottage with an iron roof, and a garden with a few red dahlias and some cosmea in it. The boarding house keepers are far too busy to have a moment in the summer to think of gardens. I have a clean little bedroom, which is all I ask.

The dining-room – well, it is of the old familiar pattern in these parts, rejoicing in the class of decoration that I suppose came to fill up the gap when the early Victorian wax flowers and fruit under shades began to go out. One of those wonderful coloured-paper affairs hangs from the ceiling – rosettes and streamers, and so on – I've never been very clear whether these are meant as fly-traps or mammoth shaving-balls, or lamp-shades, do you know? Item, a vase of dyed pampas grass; item, a pyramid of sea-eggs; item, two ornate clocks, stopped, of course; item, coloured glass vases, never filled with flowers; item, a cheap plaster figure of a fat girl on tip-toe, with the corner of her dress in her hand, and the word 'Spring' wickedly carved on it to account for her; item, wall-pockets made of perforated cardboard, and palm fans, also with pockets on them, empty of everything, of course, but dust; item, a jar covered with bits of broken china; item, 'crazy patchwork' cushions.

The mantelpiece and fireplace are swathed and draped with an inconceivable number of yards of art muslin trimmed with irrelevant tassel fringes.

Oh, to be a new Savonarola, and with burning words persuade the owners of rooms like this to bring out all their fripperies and meaningless ornamentations, and cast them on a bonfire! I am writing on and on, just for the urgent need of talking to someone. At the best of times I never make friends easily, and in my present mood I simply *can't* be interested in the other women here, or even talk to them much. They are all in the above-described dining-room, and three of them are doing shadow-work, pillow-shams and mats, and the other is reading aloud – *The Family Herald*. So I'm writing on the dressing-table by Boy's bedside, and I have no doubt whatever they are congratulating themselves that silent, sour-tempered Mrs Courtney has taken herself off to bed. And yet I'm lonely, horribly lonely and homesick – though you needn't tell Alan so. The night silences on the mountain are like no other silences I know. And I sit and sit, watching Baby sleeping, fancying he is looking paler and more wasted; fancying, with a throbbing heart, that he is hardly breathing at all, that something has happened, till if a moth flutters in the room, or the window creaks, I could shriek aloud.

I had a long, bright letter from Esther yesterday. She says Yarrahappini is looking its loveliest, and they are all combining to spoil her; that she lies in one of the hammocks on the verandah nearly all day, and Peter and Essie vie with each other who shall go down the orchard most often and bring her the biggest peach or apricot, and that she has been forced, owing to the flesh being weak, albeit the

spirit willing, to establish a bag, ostensibly for
sewing, but really to surreptitiously receive these
perpetual contributions of fruit which they aver will
'make you feel quite strong and well and want to
jump about like us.'

I am very glad she is having such a rest, Nell, I
often think we haven't half appreciated dear old
Esther as we ought to have done. Just think of her
as she was when she 'married us' – twenty and
hardly a wish denied her in all her life. She was the
very apple of their eyes, you know, and then to take
to a rampageous lot like we were! Why, there are
times when I feel as if with my little house and one
baby I have too much to do; and she had six of
us – we were horrid little wretches too, I'm
sure – and her own baby, and big Misrule and
careless servants, and father, who is very much
more 'difficult' than Alan. And yet how bright and
full of fun she has always been – always entering
into all our games and our troubles as if she had
been one of us. Since I have had my own little
home, and the sweet privacy of life with just us two
and the little third, I think I have realised that her
lines were not cast in very pleasant places, and yet
I've never heard her grumble once, have you? At
least, just once. Do you remember years and years
ago we had all been up to some mischief or
other – I know Bunty had spoiled father's uniform,
and Judy had done something or other with the
scythe, and all the rest of us something equally bad?
Father was frightfully angry, I remember, and after
he had gone she just dropped down in the

rocking-chair and burst out crying. She sobbed, 'Seven of you and I'm only twenty, it is too bad – seven of you! Oh dear, it *is* too bad!'

She has the sweetest, sunniest, loveliest nature of any woman I ever knew or heard of.

Well, no more of my scribble tonight, dear girl. 'Mister Son' has opened his eyes, and yawned, and kicked all the clothes off, which is a signal that his bondslave is to set to work hard and prepare his last meal. By the way, could you spare me that little old Primus stove that used to stand in the second pantry? I must be a fearful nuisance to these people, penetrating into their kitchen to boil the milk, and yet Boy must be fed punctually, and the spirit-stove is so very slow. If you can unearth it – in my day Martha used it chiefly for keeping a plate of dinner warm for late-comers – pack it up and send at once. Bunty or Pip would take it to the station and book it to me.

Tell me all the home news, dearest, I do long so for post time.

Ever your sister,

MEG

Yarrahappini

DEAR OLD MEG (wrote Peter),
I hope the nipper's getting on. I nearly shot a kangaroo yesterday, only Essie went and made a row. Girls are no good to take out hunting. I'll teach the nipper how to shoot and ride and do things – don't you let anyone else teach him, 'cause I pick to. There's an old blackfellow here what

smokes and smokes, and he tells me about all the bushrangers what he's killed. He's killed thirty, that's a good lot, isn't it? When I'm as big as Pip I'm going to have a real repeating-rifle – this one grandpa lent me isn't much good – and I'm going to kill bushrangers all the time. I'm learning on rabbits, and I'll kill a good lot when Essie stops coming out with me. I'll make a rug of the skins for the nipper to crawl on.

Essie and me went up the hill on Sunday to see Judy. It makes you feel pretty bad to feel you were the one she saved, and if it hadn't been for you she could have been having fun and running about instead of lying lonely like that up there. I wish I could do something for her. I did mend the white fence, and I swept up all the leaves, and weeded the grass, and gave her all the roses I could find in the garden, but that is nothing to what she did for me.

Yours truly,

PETER

Redbank

MY WIFE, MY DARLING, MY OWN DARLING,

That is grand news about the boy. I felt certain the mountain air would set him right. Continue the medicine another week and then I think you can try him without it, and after this don't peptonise the food any longer. Kiss him for his daddie. The house looks very empty with his perambulator gone from the hall, and the cradle from the bedroom. I don't have to remove a rattle and a big shell, and some empty cotton-reels and stuffed doll, from my chair now when I go to sit down. But I think I miss the wobbly duck the most – breakfast is indeed a desolate meal, now there is no one in a high chair trying hard to give a dissipated-looking india-rubber duck a drink out of my cup by dipping its head in.

Darling, you mustn't trouble about me. I look after myself no end, and Poppet – why Poppet is better than forty aunts to me. I've never been the subject of such anxious care in all my life before. The door bell has hardly gone before she is in the room with a boiling-hot cup of coffee, and my leggings and umbrella and mackintosh, if it is at all like rain. 'Yes, you *must* put them on – for Meg's sake,' she says, and I give you my word I've worn the blessed things twice when there was no need, just to set her mind at rest. We have surprisingly nice things to eat – does the little witch cook them herself? Or is Lizzie in a conspiracy to 'tempt my appetite'? They both only giggle when I inquire. The only thing that troubles me is I don't like the child to worry herself so. She ought to be out of doors playing about, instead of sitting deep in Mrs Beeton, or hovering about to see if the waiting-room is guiltless of dust, or feeling my singlets when they come from the wash to see if they are aired, and looking preternaturally grave and responsible all the time. Write to her and tell her not to make such a little Martha of herself – she won't listen to me.

Do you know it is to Bunty I owe the fact that the Saville cheques come to me instead of Harnett! Of course I didn't learn this from the boy – it's not his way to talk, is it? – but Poppet had gathered it from

him, and she told me as a secret the other night.
When Nellie sent him for a doctor the day Enid was
burnt he got his bicycle and started off for Harnett;
and then Poppet says he thought I 'ought to have a
show' and he also felt sure 'that fellow Harnett'
wouldn't do her any good. So to make up for going
the extra mile to me while she was waiting, the lad
nearly killed himself, he rode so hard. 'Rode like
mad up the Red Hill,' Poppet said, 'and you know
how it makes your heart beat even to go
slowly – and then tore down the other side so hard
he couldn't have stopped for long enough even if
he'd wanted. And he knocked a boy down – it
didn't hurt him – and nearly ran over a dog, and a
p'leeceman ran after him, but he got to you as
quickly as anyone else could have got to that horrid
Dr Harnett, who gets all the people.' I remember
now how he fell down in the hall frightfully done
up, and how a constable came after him and
wanted to take his name, but went off satisfied
when he heard how urgent the case was. Wasn't it
decent of the lad? I shan't soon forget it.

By the way, I hope young Nell knows what she is
doing. Or does a woman ever quite know? Twynam
haunts Misrule; I have found him two or three
nights just walking up and down outside the
gate – as once I walked. If I go there to tea, I find
him there – Nell generally says, as excuse, they
simply had to ask him as he stayed so long in the
afternoon. If Nellie goes to town, he goes to town
too. I hope the child is not playing with him – he is
one of the decentest fellows I know, yet he is not

the kind of man I ever thought would attract her.

Saville's cheque for this quarter came yesterday, fifty pounds. It seems a good deal of money, but I have the consciousness that I do honestly earn it, I give the child a couple of hours every day. And I am more than pleased with her – she surpasses my most sanguine hope. In another year or two she will have caught quite up to other girls of her age, and there won't be a whit of difference between them. Indeed, now that it is clear and well, it seems to me a particularly strong, eager little mind the child has – she may make a clever woman yet. Poor Saville's delight in her is quite touching.

I shall hand the fifty pounds straight over to your father – that chips off still another piece of our millstone, darling. I wonder what we shall feel like when we are swimming without it – ready to play water leap-frog, I imagine.

Perhaps at the end of next month I shall run up to you for the Sunday.

Oh, Girlie, Girlie, it will out. The place is like a world with the sun gone out. I miss you inexpressibly every moment I am in the house, and when I am out I have all the time the dull sense hanging over me that you are not there – that when I go back and open the door I shall find that all the place is dark,

'And all the chambers emptied of delight.'

And yet the separation has done one thing – made me realise how intensely and entirely I love

you. When you were close at hand, and there was
Little Boy with us wanting our incessant care, there
seemed no time, no place, to stand back and look at
love as a thing apart. I just knew you were very, very
dear and very necessary to me. But this absence has
stirred all the old, deep feelings I used to have for
you when you were sweet Meg at Misrule, and the
sound of your voice, or the gleam of your white
dress in the old garden made my heart throb with
a feeling that was almost pain.

My Meg, my bride, my wife, goodnight!

'The Lord watch between thee and me
While we are absent from one another.'

ALAN

CHAPTER TWENTY-THREE

One More Letter

> *'Call once more before you go,*
> *Call once yet*
> *In a voice that she will know – '*

Yarrahappini

DEAREST MEG (wrote Esther),
Peter has almost broken my heart. It is all a week
ago, and still I wake sobbing in the night. On
Sunday for the first time since we have been here I
took him up the hill to see our little grave. He has
seen it before, as you know, and of course he knows
all the sad story. But that morning he seemed to
realise it all in a way he never did before. He stood
and looked and looked and looked at the little
mound, his very soul in his eyes. I tried to draw him
away, to interest him in the bush things, for I
cannot bear to sadden a child's heart too much, but
he kept straying back to the white palings, and
leaning his forehead on them and looking through.
Yet he said very little, just a few things such as 'She

was the one who jumped about the most, wasn't she? Meg says she never could keep still a second.' And in a whisper, 'Mother, I just *couldn't* lie for ever up here, no one with me.'

Of course I tried to explain the unexplainable to him, 'the resurrection of the body and the life everlasting', but I could see I had made little impression. His wet eyes saw nothing but eager little Judy leaping to death to save him, and for it, lying here year after year.

The next day we did not see him all the morning, and as he would not take Essie with him we concluded he had gone to try a harmless old gun father has given him. I found out later he had been up at the grave all the time. The grave itself is always beautifully kept, but the grass grows long and the leaves fall in the enclosure. The poor child had been working for hours, trying to clear those leaves – such a day too, the hottest I ever knew. And mother and I had both scolded him early in the day – you know how she loves and cherishes her roses – he had been down to the bushes and cut off every blossom. When we scolded him he did not say a word, and we thought he had plucked them for some game with Essie, then later we found them all laid thickly on the mound.

At night a frightful thunderstorm came up after the hot day. It rained in torrents, and the wind raged and blew as if it would bring the house down. I went into the children's room about nine o'clock, thinking they might have wakened with so much noise. Essie was sound asleep in the cot, but Peter's

bed was empty. We searched the house in alarm,
then I saw a side door open and an instinct told me
where he was. Father and I put on our
mackintoshes and got a lantern, and I ran, ran with
a throbbing heart, all the way up the hill, with the
rain in my face and the thunder crashing overhead,
and there was my poor little boy crouching beside
the grave.

'Peter,' I sobbed, as I snatched him up.

'It's all right, mother,' he said, with chattering
teeth, 'don't worry, I put my dressing-gown and
slippers on.' And so he had; the little felt slippers
were pulp; the grey gown was soaked through and
through. Father carried him down the hill, and he
sobbed all the way because we wouldn't leave him a
little longer. I undressed him and gave him a hot
bath, crying like a baby myself all the time – I felt I
could never stop again. And then I wrapped him in
a blanket and sat in a rocking-chair by the fire with
him, and he was no longer my great lad who goes
about with a gun and cracks a stock-whip, but just
my little boy baby again, cuddling up to my heart,
my little boy baby that Judy gave back to me. And
we talked in whispers to each other, and the
firelight was the only light in the room, and
gradually he told me all. How he had wakened and
been frightened at the thunder – his cheeks grew
red as he confessed this – and how he remembered
Judy was out in all the storm, lying alone, alone on
the hill-top; and how he had crept to the window
and looked out at the wild, black trees fighting with
the wind, and the clouds sweeping across the sky,

and the rain blowing in gusts at the window.

'And I thought if I just went and sat beside her a little time she wouldn't feel so dreadfully lonely,' he whispered, 'that's all, mother. It wasn't much to do for her. I called to her that I was there, and I know she heard.'

He had bronchitis the next day, which was the least I expected. Thank Heaven, it was a very light attack, and he is mending fast and is just his mischievous, noisy self again. The whole affair seems to have slipped from his mind, and he spars with Essie and cracks his whip in bed and insists upon having his gun beside him to clear twice a day.

But I am five years older for the shock, and if a door bangs I burst out crying.

Oh, Meg, Meg, the child is best where she is – little Judy, I mean – I had clear vision of that yesterday when I went up to her. She would have loved and suffered and lived as one of her nature must have done. And oh the peace, yesterday, on her hill-top, and oh the wise, tender evening sky brooding down over her, and the young stars coming out to watch, and the soft air that seems full of her.

I kissed her grass and smoothed it, and looked up to the shining stars, her eyes, and thanked God inasmuch as He had let me see that all had been for the best.

CHAPTER TWENTY-FOUR

All Awheel

'Smile the earth and smile the waters,
Smile the cloudless skies above us.'

'Never saw such a tyre,' said Bunty, 'it's as soft as squash. How do you think you're going to ride thirty miles on that?'

'I did pump it up,' said Nell. But she was quite content to leave it to brotherly ministrations, and she leisurely put on her thin gloves and settled her sailor hat, and felt happy in the consciousness that her cycling-skirt hung beautifully.

'You don't find Poppet starting off with tyres like that,' said Bunty. 'Here you've got the best bicycle that money could buy – old Saville must have given forty pounds for this "trifling Easter egg", as he calls it – and as long as the handle-bars are brilliant that's all you care.'

Nell gave him her sweetest smile. 'I'm not inconsiderate enough to deprive you of the pleasure of doing it for me,' she said.

Bunty gave a final pump. 'I could just survive the

disappointment,' he said. 'Have you got all your tools – well, I'm blessed!'

'You let my tool-bag alone,' said Nell, but Bunty over-hauled it ruthlessly.

'Just like Nell,' he said. 'I say, Pip, she's left her spanner and oil-can and wrench behind, and put in a clothes-brush and a finnicky brush-and-comb and looking-glass, and a sponge.'

'Well,' said Nellie, 'and why should one be a dust-covered object even if one does ride? I propose to borrow *your* tools if I need them.'

Bunty grinned. 'All right, and I'll borrow the looking-glass and see if my cap's straight every mile or two.'

Poppet came wheeling her bicycle down the drive; Poppet in a well-worn serge frock and a straw hat that was sunburnt and ancient to a degree, but had the merit of keeping the sky's glare from her eyes.

'Oh, Poppet,' said Nell, 'that awful hat! Why Flibberty-Gibbet was worrying it on the lawn the other night.'

Poppet put her hand to it jealously. 'What's the matter with it? It's a beautiful hat,' she said, 'you'll want to change with me before we've gone a mile,' and she looked disparagingly at her sister's neat, spotless one with its narrow brim.

Bunty looked Poppet over with pride. 'She's all right,' he said, 'and if you thought less of your hat and more of your riding you'd get along faster. You've taken three times as long to learn as Poppet did, and you still pedal like the girls who hire bikes for half-a-day, and you jam your brake down and hold back for your life down a hill no one else sees is there.'

'She's all right,' said Pip. 'Poppet gets up to too many

tricks – she'll smash herself up one of these days coasting down Red Hill, or going about with her hands off.'

Esther and Meg came down with the four light cases they had been filling with sandwiches and similar light refreshments; for the party had a thirty-mile ride down the coast before it, then it was to pass the night at the house of a country friend of the family, and ride back the next day.

By Meg's side, trotting along on his fat little legs, that he had only just begun to use for purposes of locomotion, came Little Boy. Meg and he had come to spend the day at Misrule, for Alan was to be of the bicycle party all the first day, returning, however, in time for patients the next morning.

'Hello, Mr Podsnap,' said Pip, picking up the small nephew and riding him up and down the footpath to that young person's intense satisfaction.

The group at the gate grew. Peter and Essie came pedalling down on their gay-coloured tricycles half-a-mile on their way, but they were properly equipped. Each dangled a packet of sandwiches at the handle-bars, and a luggage parcel behind them. Peter wore the tops of his stockings turned down in vain emulation of Pip, and Essie had fastened a pair of Bunty's clips to the top of her socks.

'Aren't we ready?' said Bunty impatiently. 'Always the way, half the day wasted if you take girls.'

'As it happens, it is for a member of your own noble sex we are waiting,' Nell said. 'When Alan deigns to put in an appearance we are complete.'

But she glanced down the road as if not quite satisfied with her own statement.

'Alan ran in to Enid, of course,' said Meg. 'He will not be many minutes.'

'I thought Twynam was coming,' Pip said.

Nellie began to examine the contents of her tool-bag.

'Oh, that chap doesn't know his own mind,' said Bunty. 'Asked to come on Thursday, said he didn't think he could on Friday, went in and bought a new bicycle on purpose on Saturday, and yesterday said he thought he'd stop at home.'

'Oh,' said Poppet, 'that's lucky. It's much nicer just ourselves and no strangers, isn't it, Nell?'

'Of course,' said Nell, with heightened colour.

'Well, he's changed his mind again, for here he comes,' said Pip, as a figure in grey appeared on the brow of the hill, 'and I'm not sorry, for he's got my best pump.'

Nellie began to arrange her tool-bag again with great care.

'And here's Alan at last,' said Poppet.

Down the next drive came the young doctor, all the Saville family with him – the squatter, serene and ruddy-faced, smoking, and Enid, bright-eyed and loving, hanging on to his arm; Mrs Saville beside him, looking years younger and wonderfully handsome; Lylie running to gaze at the adored Poppet; Jack on *his* tricycle to swell the smaller party.

'Thought you weren't coming,' said Bunty, as Twynam jumped off and went to shake hands with the Misrule group.

The man's colour deepened. 'I am not,' he said, 'correspondence – English mail – obliged to stay. Only ran down to return your pump, Woolcot – thought you'd need it.'

The Saville contingent had drawn near by this, and greetings passed between gate and gate. In the confusion of so many on the pathway, it was not to be wondered at that Twynam found himself near Nellie.

'So you are not coming,' she said lightly.

'The mail,' he said, 'English mail – my letters.'

'Oh yes, of course,' said Nellie. 'Aren't you foolish to have wasted time coming down with the pump – Pip has another one?'

The man's face was quite white. Nellie was moving her machine from the fence, and no one was very near.

'You know that isn't the reason,' he said. 'You know that I simply dare not, that two such days would be more than I could bear.'

Nellie bumped her bicycle into the fence, and dragged it away and wheeled it in an erratic fashion to the edge of the footpath. He followed her, manipulating his machine still more clumsily.

'I should only be in your way, shouldn't I?' he said. 'You would rather I did not come.'

Nellie put one neat foot on the pedal, and began to arrange her skirt for the saddle.

'It's an open road,' she said, 'there might be room for you, unless you ride very badly.'

The man went whiter than ever.

'Nellie,' he said, 'Nellie, it is life or death with me – don't trifle. Tell me to go back to my work, the only thing I'm fitted for.'

Nellie's hand trembled a little – the hand she was just ready to push off with as she jumped up to her saddle.

'Tell me to go back,' he repeated, his voice thick with emotion.

'I – I can't be so rude,' said Nellie, very low, very, very low.

'What?' he said, taking a giant stride after her.

But Nell, the very tips of her ears suffused with sweet,

193

shamed colour, had sprung to her saddle and gone pedalling for dear life up the hill after Bunty, who, in disgust at all the dallying, had started off with Poppet.

And now all the line of wheels was on the red road, and goodbyes were called from the gates, and the sky smiled down on the happy young faces, and all the waves of the river, left behind, laughed and leaped to catch a glimpse of them.

'I thought you weren't coming,' Bunty said, looking over his shoulder and finding Twynam riding hard behind.

'I changed my mind again,' said Twynam.

Nellie shot on ahead.

Far behind, Peter and Essie and Jack toiled at their little wheels. Sometimes they got off and pulled them along; sometimes the big bicycles waited for them to catch up, for all knew they were to be of the party as far as the cross-roads.

Further behind still, at the gate, the Major stood, and regarded his first grandchild as thoughtfully as the child regarded him. It was taking him a long time to get quite used to the relationship, but still the feeling, when the small man occasionally grasped at his leg for support, was a pleasurable one.

Meg and Esther's eyes were on the far hill where the wheels looked now like a line of large black ants. Up, up and over the brow they went one after the other, and then the puff of dust went down and the hill showed speckless.

'Well, that's the last of them,' said Esther.

'The very last,' said Meg.

The Major turned his face to the house and lent a finger to the boy.

'You've left the gate open,' he said, half way up the drive, to Meg and Esther, who had entered it before him.

But there sprang up a gust of eager wind, and the next moment the Misrule gate swung to with a crash.

About the Author

Born in England in 1870, Ethel Turner came to Australia with her widowed mother and two sisters, Lilian and Rose, when she was ten years old. She showed a great love of literature while still at school, and in her late teens she and Lilian made their first bold venture into the publishing world when they launched a literary and social magazine in Sydney.

Ethel kept diaries for a remarkable sixty-two years, recording the details of her full and eventful life. As a young girl she had a great ambition to be famous, and her dream was realised earlier than she expected when she decided to try her skill at a children's story.

In January 1893 she recorded in her diary: *Night started a new story that I shall call 'Seven Little Australians'*. Later that year, she finished the book, parcelled it up and sent it off to a publisher in Melbourne. Since then the book has sold over two million copies in the English language and has been reprinted over fifty times. It has been translated into at least eleven languages. *Seven Little Australians* was performed as a stage play in 1915; made into a film in 1939; a BBC television series in 1953; a ten-episode ABC television series in 1973 – which has been seen in twenty-four countries around the world; and more recently, was presented as a musical stage play, which had its premiere in Melbourne in 1988.

Seven Little Australians was not the only book that Ethel Turner wrote. In fact, she went on to write over forty books in her lifetime. Three of them – *The Family At Misrule, Little Mother Meg* and *Judy and Punch* – follow the lives of the Woolcot family as they grow up.

She wrote numerous short stories and poems, many of which were published in the magazines of the day, while others were compiled into collections in book form. Ethel Turner devoted forty years to encouraging and inspiring young people in their literary efforts through her weekly children's page in the *Town and Country* journal, and in 1921, giving herself the title of Chief Sunbeamer, she started 'Sunbeams', the children's supplement of the *Sun Herald* newspaper.

Ethel married Herbert Curlewis and lived in Sydney, overlooking the beautiful waters of Middle Harbour. They had two children: Jean, who later became an author like her mother, and Adrian, who followed in his father's footsteps when he became a lawyer.

When still only a young woman Jean died, and with this tragedy Ethel's writing career came to a sudden end. Her heart was broken, and her attempts to write another book were in vain, even though she lived for another twenty-eight years. Her son Adrian married, and he and his wife, Betty, had a son, Ian, and a daughter, Philippa, who has published a book all about her grandmother, called *The Diaries of Ethel Turner*.

Seven Little Australians has been read and loved by children all over the world, and has been continuously in print for over one hundred years.

Ethel Turner died in 1958, leaving as her memorial a book that is now regarded as a classic in children's literature.

MORE GREAT READING FROM PUFFIN

☆☆☆☆☆☆☆☆☆☆☆☆☆☆☆☆☆☆☆☆☆☆☆☆☆☆☆☆☆

ALSO BY ETHEL TURNER

Seven Little Australians

Children and adults have shared together their enjoyment of Ethel Turner's seven little Australians for one hundred years. Readers are welcomed into the large riverside home to meet them all, to get to know them one by one, especially Judy, the irrepressible and clever daughter who has become the loved heroine of Australians and readers in many different countries.

The Family At Misrule

The seven little Australians are now five years older. Bunty is in trouble and takes a drastic step. Pip is hiding something, and Nellie will stop at nothing to become a young lady. When Captain Woolcot and his wife set sail for India, Meg is left in charge. Who could imagine what was in store for the children . . .

Judy and Punch

From the story of *Seven Little Australians*, Ethel Turner continues Judy's adventure, from the fateful day Captain Woolcot decides to send her away to boarding school. On the steam train to the far away Blue Mountains, Judy makes friends with a lonely young boy, named Punch. Although school is challenging, Judy's longing for her family grows, until she can stay away no longer . . .

MORE GREAT READING FROM PUFFIN

☆☆☆☆☆☆☆☆☆☆☆☆☆☆☆☆☆☆☆☆☆☆☆☆☆☆☆☆

The True Story of Spit MacPhee   James Aldridge

When Spit's grandfather died, a fierce battle broke out amongst the townsfolk to decide his destiny. But tough-minded Spit wasn't going to go to any orphanage. He had plans of his own.

Winner of the 1987 Guardian *Children's Fiction Award. Winner of the NSW Premier's Literary Award.*

The True Story of Lilli Stubeck   James Aldridge

The vivid story of a proud and independent adolescent girl as she moves from poverty to wealth and back, and of her determination to retain her sense of identity whatever her environment.

Winner of the 1985 CBC Book of the Year Award.

MORE GREAT READING FROM PUFFIN

☆ ☆

Ride a Wild Pony   James Aldridge

A quarrel over a cunning Welsh pony disturbs the peace in the Australian country town of St Helen.

A Walt Disney feature film.

The True Story of Lola MacKellar   James Aldridge

Nobody in St Helen knew who Lola McKellar was – least of all Lola herself. All they knew was that she had come from a foster home in the city. So when the questions begin, Lola's security is threatened with destruction.

A Children's Book Council of Australia Notable Book, 1993.

The Broken Saddle   James Aldridge

The story of a trusting, spirited relationship between a boy and a horse and the problems with other members of the community who want to control its freedom.

MORE GREAT READING FROM PUFFIN

☆☆☆☆☆☆☆☆☆☆☆☆☆☆☆☆☆☆☆☆☆☆☆☆☆☆☆☆

Pastures of the Blue Crane   Hesba Brinsmead

A teenage Australian girl, reared in expensive schools, but without home or family, suddenly learns she has a grandfather.

Tangara   Nan Chauncy

Lexie and Merrina are friends, until Lexie is sent to boarding school and half forgets her Aboriginal companion. But dramatic events force them back into contact . . .

Nan Chauncy won the CBC Book of the Year Award three times and was awarded the Hans Christian Andersen Diploma of Merit in 1962.

A Fortunate Life   A. B. Facey

Bert Facey's account of his life has become a classic of Australian writing. The Puffin edition includes an introduction by A. B. Facey's grandson, John Rose.

MORE GREAT READING FROM PUFFIN

☆☆☆☆☆☆☆☆☆☆☆☆☆☆☆☆☆☆☆☆☆☆☆☆☆☆☆☆

All in the Blue Unclouded Weather   Robin Klein

One summer in the late 1940s, in the blue unclouded weather of the post-war years, the Melling girls are growing up. These are sisters you'll never forget.

Winner of the Children's Book Award in the 1992 NSW Premier's Literary Awards. A Children's Book Council of Australia Notable Book, 1992.

Dresses of Red and Gold   Robin Klein

It's autumn in the tiny Australian town of Wilgawa and the Melling girls are preparing for a wedding. But autumn also brings uncertainty for the Mellings – their carefree world may never be the same.